MW01611138

CHEATING THE DEVIL (SPECIAL FORCES: OPERATION ALPHA)

A DEIMOS/TRIDENT SECURITY/DELTA FORCE TEAM CROSSOVER - DEIMOS BOOK 2

SAMANTHA A. COLE

Cover designed by Judi Perkins of Concierge Literary Design
Editing by Eve Arroyo

Dear Readers,

Welcome to the Special Forces: Operation Alpha Fan-Fiction world!

If you are new to this amazing world, in a nutshell the author wrote a story using one or more of my characters in it. Sometimes that character has a major role in the story, and other times they are only mentioned briefly. This is perfectly legal and allowable because they are going through Aces Press to publish the story.

This book is entirely the work of the author who wrote it. While I might have assisted with brainstorming and other ideas about which of my characters to use, I didn't have any part in the process or writing or editing the story.

I'm proud and excited that so many authors loved my characters enough that they wanted to write them into their own story. Thank you for supporting them, and me!

READ ON!
Xoxo
Susan Stoker

AUTHOR'S NOTE

Any information regarding persons or places has been used with creative literary license so there may be discrepancies between fiction and reality. The Navy SEALs' and Delta Force operatives' missions and personal qualities within have been created to enhance the story and, again, may be exaggerated and not coincide with reality.

The author has full respect for the members of the United States military and the varied members of law enforcement and thanks them for their continuing service to making this country as safe and free as possible.

To my grandmother for giving me the love of romance.

DEIMOS

Deimos—the Greek god of terror; symbolized by the serpent; son of Ares, the god of war, and Aphrodite, the goddess of beauty and love; twin brother of Phobos, the god of fear.

The United States fought for their independence, hundreds of years ago, and won. Now, they are faced with a new fight—the one against terrorism. The government has called forth operatives, hand-picked for their skills and intelligence, to defend America's borders and shield its citizens from those who wish them harm. These men and women have willingly "died" for their country, only to be reborn under a new identity, with one common goal—to hunt, and terminate, if necessary, those hell-bent on destroying the American way of life. Joining forces with elite members of the US military, they rain terror down on their adversaries whose agendas include murdering any innocents disagreeing with their religious or political beliefs.

Enemies of the United States, there is no safe place for you to hide—Deimos will find you.

CHAPTER 1

SLOWLY PULLING DOWN THE SHEET, BRADLEY BARTON exposed his lover's bare back, then laid light kisses across her shoulder blade. Her skin was exquisite— soft, smooth, and tanned. His morning wood nestled against her thigh as he ran a hand over her shapely ass.

"Mmm. What time is it?" Avery murmured as she stirred.

He brushed his lips over her spine. "Oh-six-hundred."

"What!" The last of the covers went flying as she jumped from the bed and rushed into the master bedroom's attached bath, unfazed by her nakedness. "Brad, you were supposed to wake me earlier! We have to be at the airport by 7:30! I swear, if I'm not wearing my bikini and sipping a Mai Tai by the pool in Aruba by 2:30, you're going to be on my shit list." He heard the shower turn on, then she stuck her head back around the door jamb and pointed at him. "And that's not where you want to start our vacation."

"Yes, ma'am."

She grinned at him, then shook her head and disappeared into the bathroom again. Brad debated whether to join her but figured there'd be plenty of time for intimacy during the next seven days. How he'd gotten so lucky to have such a gorgeous, kick-ass woman interested in him was beyond comprehension. At fifty-six, he'd had more than his fair share of women over the years, but they'd been nice and sweet, with safe careers, and had eventually gotten tired of sharing their man with the United States Army. Even his ex-wife had left him shortly after their fifth anniversary, unwilling to uproot their daughter, Lori, for a transfer to yet another base— the third one in as many years. Brad hadn't been surprised when Diane had asked for the divorce, and he'd been relieved at the time. The only thing that'd hurt was the fact his visits with Lori had become few and far between. When he'd moved to Fort Hood to take a new assignment with Delta Force, they'd stayed behind in Fayetteville, North Carolina. After Diane remarried a few years later, they'd moved to Jacksonville, closer to the East Coast.

Following the divorce, Brad had run through a bunch of one-night stands, since his training and missions didn't leave him with a lot of time for anything more—at least not for a few years—and he'd been fine with that. Then, as he climbed the ranks to colonel, he'd dated a few women here and there—some lasting a few weeks, others a few months. But none of them, not even his ex-wife, could ever hold a candle to Avery Knapp.

At fifty-five, she had a petite, yet fit, body women half her age would kill for. Her shoulder-length, platinum hair was natural and highlighted the brown in her hazel eyes. She was intelligent, witty, caring, and, most of all, a bad-ass when she needed to be. At twenty-five, fluent in Mandarin, Malay, and Nepali, and about to graduate from Georgetown University with a master's degree in Asian Studies, Avery had been recruited by the CIA. After working for them for five years as a covert agent, she was then recruited to join the ranks of a new agency—one that was even more secretive. Until two years ago, Brad had never heard of Deimos—named for the Greek god of terror—and that was saying a lot, since he commanded some of the most clandestine military operatives on the planet.

He knew all too well Avery couldn't talk about most of the things she'd done over her sixteen years working as a covert operative for Uncle Sam, but he was glad that was all behind her now. Having unofficially retired from the agency—one never fully retired from black-ops agencies—she'd gotten her nursing degree and was now assigned to help another female Deimos operative recover from injuries received on a mission that had left her in a wheelchair. Unable to work in the field anymore, Haven Caldwell had been appointed to the intelligence division, working from her handicapped-accessible house, and needed someone with a high security clearance to be her aide. Avery lived in a guest house on the secure Harker Heights property that'd become Haven's home. She cooked, cleaned, and helped the younger woman with her rehab.

Ironically, some of Brad's men had been on the same mission when Haven had been shot in the back. One of them, Lucas "Frisco" Ingram, had not only rescued her but had fallen in love with her in the aftermath. It had taken a while for him to win her heart, but now the two were an engaged couple.

It was through them, and another joint mission, that Brad and Avery had met.

"Shower's all yours. Get a move on, Shrek." With a towel wrapped around her torso and another around her wet hair, Avery gave him a flirtatious wink, before reaching for the clothes she'd left out on a chair that sat in the corner of the bedroom. He loved the private nickname she'd given him since, at six foot three, he towered over her by a good eleven inches. She never used the moniker around others, for which he was grateful. The nickname he'd been given by his fellow Delta operatives, years ago, was "Tank," but with his current rank, there were few people at Fort Hood who used it.

"Yes, ma'am!" He tossed the sheets aside, unashamed he was still semi-hard. It wasn't anything she hadn't seen before over the past four months since they'd started dating.

About fifty minutes later, they pulled into the parking lot of the Killeen-Fort Hood Regional Airport as Avery disconnected the phone call she'd been on. Brad turned off the engine and glanced at her. "Roxie's okay?" he asked, having caught a few tidbits of her conversation with Haven.

"Yeah, Haven said she's mopey, probably just missing me. This is the first time I'll be leaving her behind for more than a few hours." Roxie was her golden retriever/border collie mix she'd left in Haven and Frisco's care. The Delta operative had moved into his fiancée's home last month after he and his team had returned from a three-month mission overseas.

Pulling the handle to open the driver's door, Brad smiled. "She'll probably give me an attitude when we get back for taking you away."

"Nah. She loves you too much. You spoil her rotten with treats. And don't deny it; I see you sneaking them to her all the time."

"Hey, bribery works. She's not climbing between us on the couch or in bed anymore."

Avery laughed as she got out of the SUV and met him at the tailgate. He retrieved their suitcases and locked the vehicle. Taking the two smaller, carry-on bags, he sat them on top of the larger suitcases, then wheeled all four toward the small, private terminal. A friend of his, Randall Munro, had his own four-seater plane and had volunteered to fly them to Houston where they'd catch a commercial flight to the island. The guy had family in the city, so he often flew down there to visit, and Brad had taken him up on the offer.

After settling Avery into a seat inside the

terminal and leaving the bags with her, he went out the back door in search of Randy. Brad spotted the man doing a preflight checklist on the plane a short distance away, at the same time Randy looked up and noticed him. The pilot flashed his five fingers three times indicating he needed another fifteen minutes. Since they'd gotten there early, Brad had expected that and gave his friend a thumbs-up.

Stepping back into the terminal, Brad pulled out his cell phone and found the number he wanted, then waited for the call to be picked up.

"Bryson." Captain Keane "Ghost" Bryson was one of the Delta Force officers serving under Brad's command.

"Captain, it's Colonel Barton."

"Good morning, sir. Are you on your way to Aruba yet?"

He stared out the window as another plane took off with a roar from the main runway a mile away from the private terminal. "Just got to the airport and we've got a few minutes, so I figured I'd check in. Anything I need to know about?"

Bryson gave him an update on a few things that had popped up over the last fifteen hours since Brad had left the base to start his leave. There was nothing pressing on the agenda, and even if there were, his men could handle it. They were the best of the best, and he trusted them implicitly. "All right. Sounds good. I spoke to Colonel Sheppard last night. Notify him if anything comes up. I'll also be checking in during the week."

"Always have to have one foot on the base, huh? Everything will be fine, sir. Enjoy your vacation and your woman."

Those last two words had him glancing over his shoulder to see Avery reading her Kindle, and he felt a stirring in his groin. Her hair was in a stylish bob that framed her pretty face. She'd chosen to wear a red, short-sleeved, Jersey-knit dress, that stopped just above her knees, and white, canvas, slip-on shoes for the five-and-a-half-hour trip to the island. Not for the first time in the last few days, he wondered what her bikini looked like since she wouldn't let him see it until they got there. She really was a gorgeous woman no matter what setting or clothing she was in. And once again, he wondered how he'd gotten so lucky this late in life. "Thanks."

Disconnecting the call, he made two more quick check-ins with other officers before striding back over to Avery. She lifted her head and smiled at him. "Everything okay?"

He took the seat next to her and tucked his

phone into the thigh pocket of his khaki cargo pants. "Sounds like it. You know, it's been so long since I took an actual vacation, I can't help but feel everything will go to shit if I'm not ten minutes from the base."

Smiling seductively, she set her hand on his thigh and squeezed. "Don't worry, Shrek, you'll remember how to enjoy yourself. I'll do everything I can to make sure you do."

"Yeah?" He asked while raising a brow.

"Uh-huh." Leaning closer, she brushed her lips against his. "Everything."

"Have mercy, woman."

"Never."

CHAPTER 2

WHEN THE HUGE BOEING 777 LEVELED OFF, AVERY HIT the button that would recline her first-class seat a little bit and took another sip of the champagne she'd been given prior to takeoff. Having a friend who worked in the executive offices of the airline had its perks. Avery flew first class for coach fares almost every time she went somewhere, which wasn't often. Back when she'd worked as a field operative for the CIA, and then Deimos, she'd traveled all over the world on a regular basis, but since her semi-retirement, she'd only flown within the fifty states, depending on where she was needed.

After burning out as an operative, which wasn't uncommon after twenty years of service, she'd decided to go into nursing. Yes, it had been a dramatic turnaround, going from espionage and assassinations to helping people heal from injuries or deal with a medical issue, but it'd been time for her to move on. She'd had too much blood on her hands and saving lives instead of taking them gave her a sense of atonement. While she'd never killed an innocent person, she still regretted every time she'd had to end someone's life, even if it was to ensure the safety of the citizens of the United States.

Glancing at Brad doing the Killeen Daily Herald's crossword puzzle from yesterday's Sunday edition, she smiled to herself. It was one of the habits she'd learned he had over the past few months. He didn't do the smaller daily ones, saying most of them were too easy, but the Sunday puzzles were larger and more challenging. After he completed it, he'd move onto the Jumble and Sudoku puzzles, and then the cryptograms. Usually he did them after breakfast on Sundays, over a cup of coffee or two, but had saved this week's puzzles for the trip. The man had brains *and* brawn, which, combined with a sense of humor, alpha presence, gentleness, and good looks, had drawn her to him the first few times they'd met, before he finally asked her to dinner one night. If he hadn't, she'd been close to asking him out, but had held off as an unaccustomed shyness had come over her whenever he'd been around. Never in her life had she been tongue-tied in a man's presence, nor did she blush often, but Bradly Barton gave her the butterflies in her stomach that hadn't been there since she'd been a teenager. Every time he'd aimed his steel-gray gaze at her, her body responded in the way nature intended when two people were attracted to each other. And when he'd winked and smiled seductively at her, her knees had turned to jelly and she'd grow wet from wanting him.

Reaching up, she brushed her fingers across the nape of his neck, where his salt-and-pepper hair was barely an eighth of an inch long. It was longer on the top, but still Army regulation length. He hadn't shaved this morning, telling her she should prepare herself for some whisker burns on her inner thighs this week. He usually didn't shave on the weekends, but she'd never seen him with more than a two-day beard, which just enhanced his good looks, in her opinion. From the appreciative looks he got from females of all ages, wherever they went, Avery wasn't the only one who thought he was a silver fox.

When he glanced her way, she asked, "What time are Lori and her boyfriend landing in Aruba?"

Brad let out a sigh. She knew he was happy his

daughter had agreed to join them on the island—he'd wanted the two women in his life to meet—but he was also nervous about it. Throw in the fact the twenty-four-year-old was being accompanied by the guy she'd been dating for a few months—the one who was four years older than her—and Brad was not exactly looking forward to the awkwardness that was sure to come.

"They're supposed to land about twenty minutes after us. While we're waiting, I'll get our vehicle." He paused. "I hope this kid she's bringing isn't an asshole."

"She still didn't tell you anything about him when you spoke to her last night?"

He shook his head. "Nope. All I know is he's twenty-eight and his name is Cameron. She wouldn't tell me his last name because she didn't want me investigating him before I met him. So, of course, I've got all these crazy thoughts going through my head about this guy. Does he have a prison record? Is he a drug dealer? Is he a bum that doesn't even have a job? I mean, I know she's a talented tattoo artist—not my first choice of a career for my only daughter, but it is what it is—but you never know who's going to walk into the place. The clientele can range from frat boys, to skells, gang members, and criminals, or party girls and soccer moms."

"Well, you said the place is in a nice part of town and the owner never leaves her there by herself, so it sounds like she's safe enough. I'm sure her boyfriend's a nice guy—and if he's not, between the two of us, we've got plenty of people we can call to dispose of the body."

Brad snorted then chuckled, the anxiety about meeting his daughter's beau leaving his face. "Thanks, I needed that."

"No problem. Now, finish your puzzles because when we get there, you're all mine."

The first few hours of the flight were pleasant with very little turbulence, which was the only thing Avery hated about flying. On a trip to China, early in her CIA career, she'd had a scary flight. While going through a storm, the turbulence had been so violent the aircraft had shaken and dipped up and down, overhead bins had popped open, the flight attendants had needed to be buckled in, and everyone had prayed. Avery, and every other passenger, had been white-knuckled, nauseous, and pale as a ghost until the pilot had finally gotten them through it. Ever since, at the slightest drop or shimmy of a plane, Avery's heart rate spiked, and her gut clenched. She just kept telling herself the odds of becoming the President of the United States or being struck by a meteorite outnumbered the chances of being killed in a plane crash until the moment passed.

Halfway through the flight, Brad had closed his eyes and fallen into a light sleep after eating his gourmet meal—or what passed as one on the thirty-passenger, commercial plane. Having finished Susan Stoker's latest romance-suspense novel, Avery shut off her Kindle and reclined her seat further as the flight attendant took their empty lunch trays. Reading was a luxury Avery had always treasured, finding time to dive into the latest releases by her favorite authors, or even someone new she'd discovered, whenever she had the chance. Like many readers who used fiction as a way to get away from the routine grind of daily life, Avery had long been an avid reader, especially during her active agent days. Books calmed her. After spending a mission wondering if she'd make it out alive or after she'd had to do something unpleasant, like kill someone. Then, as she'd worked her way through nursing school and her new assignments tending to the injured or ill agents from Deimos or the CIA, reading helped her escape into someone else's world for a few hours, where happily-ever-afters existed.

The one thing Avery regretted about going into the world of covert ops was not being able to find a nice guy to settle down and have children with. There had been plenty of men over the years— several one-night stands, a few agents like herself who couldn't afford to trust many others with the details of their lives, and the occasional target who had no idea Avery wasn't a clerk at the American embassy in Tokyo as she'd claimed. Hell, even her parents and the few friends from her former life thought she'd had a desk job, translating documents for the CIA—a nice, safe job, as far as they were concerned. Over the years, though, her parents had both passed away, and Avery had lost touch with her high school and college friends.

When she'd first started nursing school, it had taken her a few months to come out of the shell she'd unconsciously tucked herself into. She'd spent years constantly on guard and always assessing someone's motives for approaching her for any reason. Anyone could've been a foreign spy who'd figured out she wasn't who she'd portrayed, or, God forbid, an assassin sent to take her out. She'd forgotten what it was like to just have girlfriends to chat with and maybe go out for a bite to eat. During nursing school, she'd forged several relationships with some of the women in her classes. In fact, she'd become so close with one of them, Judi Perkins, that her daughter, Callie, called Avery her aunt. Not long after Avery had taken the position of helping Haven, about a year ago, Judi's husband had been transferred to Fort Hood, so the two friends had been thrilled they could see each other whenever they wanted again.

"Passengers and flight attendants, please prepare for landing."

With that announcement, Brad woke up immediately. Being in the military, and special ops at that, he could fall asleep and wake up completely refreshed at the drop of a hat. Avery used to be able to do the same, but her body had lost that conditioning over the past few years. She could if she needed to, but her catnaps were few and far between now.

It didn't take long after the announcement for them to land at the main airport in Aruba. Unlike the terminals back in Houston, the planes here did not pull up to a gate with a passageway connecting them. Instead, a long staircase was wheeled up to the cabin door, and the passengers descended into the fresh air and walked a short distance across the tarmac to the terminal. It was eighty-five degrees, sunny, and humid, and Avery was grateful she'd used her favorite anti-frizz hair cream that morning. If she hadn't, her hair would be twice as full as it was.

When they reached the tarmac, Brad reached over and took Avery's hand in his. As always, when this man touched her, the nerves under her skin tingled. In some ways, she wished she'd met Brad years ago, but then he might not have been the same man she was falling in love with. The notion that she loved him had startled her when she'd realized it about a month ago, and she still didn't have a clue if that love was reciprocated. Neither one had said the word to the other, but she knew he felt something strong toward her since he'd told her he'd never introduced a woman he was dating to his daughter before. Avery hoped she and the younger woman liked each other because she knew, even though they rarely had a chance to see each other, Lori and her approval meant a lot to Brad.

As they entered the terminal, a blast of air conditioning cooled the perspiration that'd formed on Avery's skin during the short walk from the plane. The building wasn't large, compared to its US counterparts, and everything—car rentals, waiting areas, check-in counters, and baggage claim—were all in full view. To their right, there was a VIP lounge. Large mirrors on the wall next to the door were probably one-way glass—those inside the lounge could see out, while those outside could only see the main area of the terminal reflecting back at them.

Avery and Brad joined the rest of the passengers from their flight at baggage claim. They could see out on the tarmac that the plane's cargo area was still being unloaded. Avery looked up at Brad. "Why don't you go get our car? I'll wait here for the bags. Then we can load them up and come back in to wait for Lori and Cameron."

"Sounds good. I'll be right back." Before walking away, he leaned down and gave her a gentle kiss, which Avery felt all the way to her toes. Damn, he turned her on.

It was a few minutes before the carts with their luggage arrived, and after finding hers and Brad's, Avery added them to their two carry-ons. A few feet away was a row of stationary chairs, and she wheeled the four pieces over to them and took a seat to wait for him. She took a few moments to people watch—something she always did, but not for the same reasons others did—it was instinct for her to assess who was around her and to look for anyone or anything out of place.

A tingling caused the hairs on the back of her neck to rise, and not the same tingling she'd felt when Brad had taken her hand or kissed her. Acting nonchalantly, Avery stood again, then did a slow three-sixty, trying to figure out who or what was causing her inner "oh, shit" radar to spike. No one appeared to have her in their sights, nor did anyone seem to be a threat—to Avery or anyone else. There were several uniformed security officers walking about, but none were alarmed by anything. Arriving and departing passengers milled about, and airline personnel were performing their assigned jobs. Avery glanced at the VIP lounge but couldn't see anyone inside.

"You okay, sweetheart?"

She turned to face Brad. "Yeah. Just getting a weird vibe in here."

He frowned and glanced around, not even questioning what she meant. That was one of the good things about dating someone in special ops—he didn't need her to explain things when it came to moments like this. "Anyone out of place?"

"No. Maybe my Spidey-sense is off."

They both took in their surroundings, but after

several more moments without anyone standing out, Avery shrugged. "I must be mistaken."

"Brad!"

The young woman's voice calling his name caught their attention. Beside Avery, Brad smiled. "Hey, sweetheart. How was your flight?"

Lori Barton was five foot eight, with a slender figure. Her long, honey-brown hair was pulled up into a ponytail, and her gray eyes were exactly like her father's. Dressed in white capri pants and a navy-blue tank top, she proudly showed off her full sleeve of tattoos on her left arm. A colorful butterfly adorned her right ankle just above her navy flip-flops. Brad had warned Avery that Lori had been calling him by his first name since she'd hit the rebellious age of fourteen. It irked him, but he'd learned to pick his battles with his daughter a long time ago—especially when he only got to see her a few short weekends a year. At least she called her stepfather by his first name too—although it was a small consolation.

As the father and daughter hugged each other, Avery turned her attention to the young man who stood waiting to be introduced. She smiled at him. "Cameron?"

"Yes, ma'am." If his polite response hadn't clued

her into the fact he was in the military, his tightly shorn, black hair and proud stature sure did. His brown eyes also didn't seem to miss a thing about their surroundings.

Avery held out her hand. "It's nice to meet you. I'm Avery Knapp."

"Cameron McGee," he clarified as he shook her hand. "It's a pleasure, ma'am."

Lori stepped back from Brad. "Cam, this is my dad, Brad." She gave her father a reproachful glare. "This is Cameron. Be nice."

Brad frowned. "When am I not nice?"

"When you're being the colonel or glaring at any man who dared to eye your daughter."

"It's my job, little girl."

"Brad," Lori responded with a huff. "I'm not a little girl anymore. I haven't been for a while."

Reaching up, he tugged on her ponytail. "You'll always be my little girl, even when you have one of your own." Brad waved at Avery to step closer. "Lori, this is Avery."

"Hi. My dad told me all about you." Avery was certain Brad hadn't told his daughter quite every-thing but, of course, she didn't mention that. "It's nice to finally meet you."

"Same here. I'm so glad you both could join us

for a few days."

Brad reluctantly extended a hand to her boyfriend, who returned the gesture. "Cameron, what branch and rank are you?"

The young man didn't appear fazed by the curt greeting, which earned him a few more points in Avery's eyes. "Marine Corps, sir. Corporal. Based out of Camp Lejeune."

He nodded, not showing any signs of being impressed or cordial. "Brigadier General MacAskie's command?"

"Yes, sir. He's a good commander."

"That he is. What's your assignment?"

Before Cameron could respond, Lori rolled her eyes and interrupted, "Can we save the interrogation for later, please? There's a piña colada calling my name at the hotel, and it would be rude to not answer."

Avery grinned, and, after a moment, Brad followed suit. "Fine. Avery's been craving a Mai Tai, so let's get your bags and go."

Five minutes later, all their luggage collected, the foursome was walking out the door toward where their rental was waiting, but not before Avery glanced back over her shoulder one more time, still feeling like she was being watched.

CHAPTER 3

LIN CHAO SIPPED HIS SPARKLING WATER AS HE WAITED in a comfy, leather seat located in the VIP lounge. His private jet should have already been in the air, heading for Malaysia, but there'd been a minor maintenance issue that needed to be addressed. After reaming the pilot for not being ready, he'd stepped back into the terminal and headed for the lounge, trailed by his bodyguard who now stood sentry nearby. Instead of watching the news or golf game being shown on the two wide-screen TVs hanging above the bar, Chao stared out the window separating the elite from the peasants scurrying around the main terminal. People watching was something he always found fascinating, ever since he'd been a little boy, growing up in an impoverished town in Northern China. He'd always tried to guess who the travelers passing through were and what their station in life was. It wasn't until he was twelve, after his parents had died—his father in a mining accident, his mother of a grief-induced suicide shortly after—that Chao realized how poor his family had been. He'd been taken in by a neighbor after his mother's death, but several days later, two men arrived and announced they were taking Chao to live with his grandfather. The wealthy man hadn't approved of his daughter's choice of a husband and had disowned her when she'd refused to enter into an arranged marriage.

It wasn't long before Chao had been getting a full education, catching up on the subjects his poor school hadn't focused on. He'd gone from wearing stained and torn clothing to being dressed in the finest attire available—he'd even taken his maternal surname as his own, discarding the last connection to the pathetic man who'd sired him. At his grandfather's side, he'd learned the family business—Chao was the only living male heir the elderly man had after his son's wife had only produced two females. Being extremely wealthy, the family had been allowed to have more than one child amid the country's strict population laws.

After his grandfather passed away, twenty-five-year-old Chao had taken over the conglomerate the old man had created. Then the heir had made the family business bigger and better, albeit less legal. With cultivated connections in the government, Chao skirted the laws of the land. Because he'd padded their pockets, and created jobs for the peons, the officials looked the other way. At least, most of them did. There had been several he hadn't been able to turn, and at least one of them had been the cause of the demise of Chao's businesses. Now here he was, banished from his homeland, his empire and family in ruins.

A new influx of tourists entered the terminal, and Chao studied each one. A tall man with a commanding presence towered over several other people, but as the small crowd thinned, it was the petite woman at his side who drew Chao's attention. Rage boiled within him as every muscle in his body went rigid. His hands clenched. She was older than the last time he'd seen her, but he knew without a doubt he was staring at the woman who'd killed his eldest son. The fifteenth anniversary of Delan's death was approaching, but Chao still felt the loss as if it'd happened only yesterday. He'd been cheated out of revenge all those years, but with that murdering bitch walking into his territory, all vows he'd made to those in power in his homeland, in exchange for his freedom, were off the table now.

Chao snapped his fingers, prompting his bodyguard and right-hand man, Shao Yan, to approach. Aware of his surroundings, the old man kept his voice low and spoke in his native tongue. "That woman in the red dress. Find out where she and her companions are going—discreetly. I want to know everything you can find out about her." As Yan strode toward the door to the main terminal to do his bidding, Chao picked up his cell phone and called his driver, who'd dropped them off less than thirty minutes ago. When the call was answered, Chao ordered, "Come back to the airport to pick me up. My plans have changed." Without waiting for an answer, he disconnected the call and glared at the woman who would never leave the island alive.

LYING IN A CHAISE LOUNGE, SWIRLING THE STIRRER IN her Mai Tai, Avery chuckled at Brad, who was glaring at two couples chatting in the pool. The sun was deliciously warm, and Avery was fast on her way to getting the darker tan she'd been looking forward to. Her navy-blue bikini was a bit more conservative than Lori's black and white one, yet still showed off the curves the older woman worked hard to maintain. She wasn't as solid as she'd been twenty years ago and had added about twenty pounds to her petite frame since then, but she still garnered appreciative glances from men of all ages. It was a boost to her ego, but there was only one man she was interested in attracting, and he was lying right next to her —brooding. Avery took a sip of her drink, then swallowed the cool, fruity liquid. "He seems like a nice guy."

With his arms crossed over his bare chest, above his flat abs and dark green swim trunks, Brad growled. "If he was a nice guy, he wouldn't have his hands all over my daughter." That was an exaggeration since the two were standing side by side in three feet of water, Cameron's arm wrapped around Lori's waist, his hand resting on her opposite hip. The other young couple they'd just met were similarly positioned, facing them. From their body language, it was obvious they were talking about the tattoos running down Lori's arm, and the other woman was considering getting a colorful sleeve too.

Avery reached over and ran a seductive finger down Brad's thick bicep. "He's not doing anything to her you didn't do to me when we were in the pool a little while ago. In fact, if memory serves, your hands were a lot busier under the water."

Finally, pulling his gaze away from the foursome, he turned his head toward her. "That's different."

"Why? Because we're older? She's twenty-four, he's twenty-eight, and they've been dating for six months. I'm sure they've moved beyond hand holding by now. You and I moved beyond that after our second date, and you were in my bed at the end of the third." Yeah, he'd swept her off her feet quickly, not that she was complaining. Sex with Brad had been better than she'd dreamed of, and she'd been dreaming of it from the moment she'd met him at Haven's house during a joint mission between his Delta teams and Deimos.

"Please don't insinuate my daughter's having sex with that punk. As far as I'm concerned, she's still a virgin and she'll stay that way until I'm dead and buried."

"Ha! Good luck with that. Just be happy he seems to treat her right."

"Seems to. It's probably an act to impress me."

Avery squeezed his upper arm. "It would take a lot more than that to impress you, and I'm sure he knows it. Just don't hold the fact he's a Marine against him. Don't turn it into an inter-branch pissing match. It's obvious they're smitten with each other. As long as she's happy, that's all that should matter."

Brad took a deep breath and let it out slowly. "All right. I'll give him a chance. But at the first sign of trouble, I'm gonna find a shovel."

Swinging her legs off the chaise, she stood and held out her hand. "Come on, Shrek. Let's go back to our room and take a nap before dinner."

"A nap?" he asked incredulously as his eyes narrowed.

"I was being discreet."

A wide grin spread across his face as he took her hand and got to his feet. "Sorry, didn't realize we'd switched into mission mode."

"Tsk-tsk. And you call yourself a Delta."

As if they'd been created with identical minds, both Avery's and Brad's eyes narrowed as they saw the small piece of clear tape they'd placed at the top of their hotel room door, where it met the jamb, had been disturbed. It was a covert operative's trick to let them know if anyone had entered their room while they were gone. Nobody should have been in there at all because they'd requested to "go green," meaning they didn't want or need daily maid service. They'd call the front desk if they needed the towels, toiletries, or sheets replaced. Whoever had gone into their room was probably a resort staff member, but since neither Brad nor Avery were one-hundred percent sure, it was better to be safe than sorry.

Because they'd taken a commercial flight onto a non-US island, neither had brought a weapon with them—not that it mattered. There were many other weapons that could be mistaken for simple, everyday items and could easily be brought onto a plane or found lying around—an operative learned to improvise and use anything and everything available to them.

Glancing around, Brad spotted a discarded room-service tray a few doors down. In silence, he hurried over and swiped the butter knife. It wasn't sharp, but with enough strength behind it, the utensil could do some damage. Meanwhile, Avery had pulled a seemingly innocent, compact umbrella, with a thicker-than-normal shaft, from her beach bag and unscrewed the handle. An expandable, tactical baton slid from inside the hollow, metal tube. With a flick of her wrist, it was ready to use.

The corners of Brad's mouth ticked upward at her ingenuity, even though it didn't surprise him. "Nice," he murmured just loud enough for her to hear.

Not caring about what hotel security thought of them if they were watching the couple on the hallway cameras, Avery and Brad stood on either side of the door to their room. Brad held the keycard to the scanner and waited for the green light to appear. There was no way to silently enter the room with the bulky handle and noisy lock, so he didn't hesitate to push open the door, using his foot to hold it ajar. When seconds passed, and no one rushed out or fired on them, the couple eased around both sides of the jamb and entered the room, letting the door shut behind them. A quick inspection revealed no one was lying in wait to murder or attack them. Nothing seemed out of place, nor did Brad have the feeling their belongings had been disturbed.

Coming out of the bathroom, where he'd checked behind the shower curtain, Brad heard Avery chuckle. "Damn room service. She's gonna be pissed—I better not tell her."

His gaze went to the huge fruit, cheese, and wine basket, which hadn't been there earlier, sitting on the glass and wicker table for two by the window.

Someone from room service must have come in while they were gone and left it. Avery stood next to the table, with a little, white card in her hand. He raised an eyebrow at her as he dropped the butter knife onto the dresser next to the wide-screen TV. "Haven?"

"Yup . . . Frisco too. Although I'm sure they intended for it to be here when we first arrived." She read from the card, "Enjoy your trip and stay out of trouble."

Tossing the card onto the table, Avery poked through the items in the basket before selecting an oversized, plump, chocolate-covered strawberry and sliding the luscious morsel from the clear plastic surrounding it. When she took a bite of it, red juice rolled down her chin. Before she could wipe it away with her hand, Brad swooped in, leaned down, and used his tongue to lap it up, reveling in the combined flavor of the fruit and Avery. Grasping her hips and pulling her close, he continued to kiss and lick his way to her mouth. He had no idea what had happened to the rest of the strawberry, and didn't care, when Avery's arms went around his neck. Her lips parted, granting his tongue entry. Strawberry, chocolate, and the spicy, feminine taste he'd always associate with the woman in his arms tantalized his palate. He moaned and deepened the kiss, while pivoting and walking her backward toward the bed. He couldn't explain it, but Avery turned him on faster than any other woman he'd ever met, and that was saying a lot. His cock was ready to explode, and they were both still dressed. Not bad for a guy in his midfifties. While his response time had started to slow down in recent years, he still didn't need the help of one of those little, blue pills. The sex-after-fifty gods were still smiling down on him.

Avery's hands dropped to the hem of the T-shirt Brad had pulled on as he'd let Lori and Cameron know they'd meet them later for dinner, before heading back to the room. Brad reached back, grabbed a handful of cotton, and yanked the shirt up and off. Avery's hands were roaming his taut abs and trim waist before his shirt hit the floor. While he rarely went into the field anymore, usually remaining at a base or camp, doling out orders, Brad kept up a daily physical fitness routine to stay in shape. It was similar to the one he'd performed during his days as an active Delta operative, although, not as strenuous as it had been back then. His joints had taken a beating over the years and let him know it more often than not lately.

Taking a step back, Brad let his gaze caress every

inch of Avery's body before reaching out and tugging on the knot holding her sarong around her hips. It took a moment before the navy and white fabric fell to the floor, pooling at her bare feet. He wasn't sure when she'd kicked off her sandals, but it didn't matter. Her feet were as petite as the rest of her, her toenails painted hot pink. Her legs already seemed tanner than when they'd first arrived in Aruba, and the scent of the coconut suntan lotion she'd used tickled his nose. His gaze trailed upward until it met her own. Avery raised her hands to the nape of her neck and untied the bikini top, then did the same to the strings that went around to her back, before letting the skimpy scrap of material drop to the floor. Brad swallowed hard as he did every time he watched her undress, wondering how in the hell he'd gotten so damn lucky this late in life.

CHAPTER 4

"Like what you see, big boy?" Avery teased Brad as his hungry gaze roamed her body while she got rid of the bikini bottoms, adding it to the growing pile of clothes on the floor. His swim trunks dropped too, releasing his thick erection. Her man was nicely built in more ways than one.

"Damn straight, woman. C'mere." He wrapped his arm around her waist and pulled her against his hard body. His mouth descended on hers again as he skillfully lowered her to the bed, holding the majority of his weight on his forearms. His kiss was lazy yet dominant, as if he had all the time in the world to convince her to submit to him—not that it ever took much convincing. They weren't in the BDSM lifestyle like some people they knew, but there was nothing wrong with letting her lover take command or engage in a little "slap and tickle." A few times, Avery had let Brad use a set of furry handcuffs she'd won during a friend's Passionate Nights party. Even though she trusted him fully, she knew how to easily get out of them without the key that'd come in the package. Another of those ingrained habits that would never die.

Sliding to the side, Brad left her mouth and kissed his way down her neck and collarbone, until he reached the swell of her breast. His fingers plucked her nipple until it peaked for him, then sucked it into his mouth. Avery squirmed under him, her hand palming the back of his head. Not for the first time, she wished his hair was a little longer, so she could tug on it.

While he worshiped her breasts, with his facial hair rasping against her skin, his hand dragged down her abdomen to her mound. His fingers toyed with the trim hairs below her clit, before continuing lower. After testing her wetness, he grasped her hips and moved her further up the bed. When they'd first started having sex, Avery had been a little embarrassed that menopause had made things a little . . . well, different down there from when she was younger, but Brad had never made her feel inadequate. He'd just smile and say that it was times like these that'd made K-Y a top seller. There was nothing wrong with growing older.

Dipping his head between her legs, he ran his tongue between her plump labia, moaning as he did so. Avery spread her thighs wider, giving him more room to tease and tantalize her. He alternated between flattening his tongue and gliding up her pussy to flicking her clit, and stiffening his tongue and impaling her with it. Her pelvis undulated—trying to get closer to his mouth even though it was impossible. He nipped her hip. "Where's the lube, baby?"

Avery gasped for air. "Right behind you . . . night stand."

Rolling into a sitting position, he snatched the small bottle she'd placed there along with several other items she liked having nearby while she was in bed. Brad was back in an instant, flipping the top of the bottle up and pouring some of the lubricant on her mound, where it trickled down between her legs. After returning the bottle to where he'd gotten it, Brad ran his fingers through the slick liquid, spreading it around and in her pussy. Within moments, Avery felt the tingling sensation and heat worthy of a five-star review for K-Y.

While he stroked and finger-fucked her, Brad watched Avery's face. He'd told her he enjoyed doing that because the changes in her expression clued him in to what she liked the most. Whatever the reason, it worked, because the man could play her like a fine violin. He plunged his fingers deep inside her, searching for the spot that would send her flying. Avery's eyelids fell as she bit her lip and arched her back. Her orgasm rushed to the surface and exploded. She cried out as her thighs clamped shut, holding Brad's hand in place as his fingers continued to move inside her. His thumb settled on her clit, stimulating her from the outside. The combination drew out her pleasure until she was completely spent.

"You're gorgeous when you cum, baby. Fucking gorgeous." Brad crawled up beside her, then rolled her on top of him, steadying her with his hands at her waist. She straddled his hips, then stacked her hands on his chest and pushed herself up onto her knees. After they'd both gotten a clean bill of health, they'd forgone the condoms; Avery didn't need to worry about getting pregnant anymore. Brad told her more than once how he loved taking her with nothing between them—something he, apparently, hadn't done with a woman since his marriage.

Reaching between her legs, Brad held his rigid cock upright for her, allowing her to ease down and take him deeply within her. This time, it was his eyes that slammed shut, as she enveloped him in her wet heat. "God, woman, what you do to me!"

Avery smiled, pleased at his guttural tone as much as his words. Lifting herself up and plunging down again, she rode him at a near-frantic pace. Her nails lightly scored his chest, the coarse hairs there tickling her fingers. From below, Brad jacked his hips, trying to go as deeply as he possibly could. The sound of flesh slapping against flesh mingled with their combined gasps, moans, and occasional curses.

Without warning, he held her tightly and rolled them again until she was underneath him. Cupping the back of one of her thighs, he bent her leg toward her chest. Picking up his pace, he fucked her hard. Avery wrapped her free leg around his hip, digging her heel into his ass, urging him on. Perspiration coated their bodies. A vein at Brad's temple pulsed. Her inner walls began to quiver around him as he pounded into her. "Cum for me again, baby. Take me with you this time."

Brad's pelvic bone repeatedly hitting her clit was her undoing this time. Fireworks ignited in her mind a split second before her world exploded. "Oh! Shii-iiitttt!"

He thrust once, twice, then held himself there, roaring his own release. Feeling him fill her, prolonged her own climax, then she melted into a satiated and blissful puddle.

Panting, Brad collapsed on top of Avery, before rolling them both onto their sides, still joined intimately. He kissed the tip of her nose. "You're going to be the death of me one day, woman, but what a helluva way to go."

LIN ZHENG WAS SURPRISED TO SEE HIS FATHER PACING in the younger man's office when he returned later that afternoon. Lin Chao was supposed to be over the Pacific Ocean by now, not at the successful resort Zheng owned and ran. The older man had supplied the backing for the venture but hadn't wanted to oversee the day-to-day operations. And Zheng knew why. While it made plenty of money for the family, it wasn't close to what Chao's former empire had been worth. An empire built on criminal activities. The Chinese government had seized a vast majority of the elder Lin's holdings before banishing him from the only land he'd ever lived on, but there had still been many accounts on foreign soil he'd been able to hold on to.

Looking back on his life as a child, Zheng often wondered where he would be right now if it hadn't been for Delan's death. His older brother had been their father's chosen one—the son who would carry on the family's legacy. However, after Delan had been killed, his parents had drowned in a sea of grief. They couldn't deal with raising their remaining eleven-year-old son—he was a constant reminder of what they'd lost. Zheng was sent to continue his education with Xian De, a revered Shaolin Monk. Master Xian had instilled upon Zheng the difference between right and wrong— something he and his brother had never learned from their father. Zheng remained with Master Xian until his eighteenth birthday and then went to university to get his degree in business administra- tion, despite the fact his father had been exiled from China. Chao and his wife had moved to the Philip- pines where they lived until Zheng graduated. The family reunited in Aruba, where they'd spent the next sixteen years building Trade Winds Resort into a successful vacation destination.

"Father, why are you not on the plane?" he asked,

using the Mandarin tongue the older man preferred over one of the four main dialects spoken by most on the island. Although the official languages of Aruba were Papiamento and Dutch, many of the island's inhabitants also learned English and Spanish in school.

"Plans changed. The time has come. Revenge shall be mine!" Chao shook his fist in the air as if in triumph.

Zheng narrowed his eyes as he closed the door behind him, not wanting his staff to hear the angry rantings of the old man. "What are you talking about?"

"She's here. That murdering bitch is on the island!"

Feeling the blood drain from his face, Zheng rounded his desk and sat in the brown, leather executive chair. He knew who his father was speaking of —there was only one female who could bring about the amount of rage now coloring the elder Lin's face —but he feigned ignorance. "Who is here?"

"Don't play dumb, boy; I raised you better than that." Actually, the man had barely raised him at all. "The cunt who killed your brother is on this island, and I'm going to make sure she never leaves it alive."

Zheng paled. "You swore you would leave her

alone." It was one of the many deals Chao had needed to make with the Chinese government, in order to stay out of prison, after his empire had collapsed following the assassination of his eldest son.

"I vowed I wouldn't go after her—I've kept my promise. But now . . ." Chao sneered as he stopped next to the huge, floor to ceiling window behind his son's desk and looked out at the blue horizon. ". . . now, she has come to me."

Fuck. Zheng ran a hand down his face as he imagined the shit storm that was coming. "Are you sure it's her?"

His father glared at him. "I will never forget the face of the woman who killed my first-born son."

Who was apparently the only important son. I never mattered.

"Why risk what we have here . . . what we've worked so hard to build?" He knew it was useless to try reasoning with the old man, but he did it anyway. "Can't you just let it go?"

Without warning, Chao backhanded him across the face, the impact thunderous in the large room. Pain bloomed through Zheng's cheek and nose as his head snapped to the side. Chao was unapologetic as he growled. "I will never 'let it go.' It is my *duty* to avenge Delan's death. It is yours too. When the time is right, you will be ready to do your part."

Chao spun on his heel and strode across the room with more energy than Zheng had seen from him lately. He didn't bother looking back as he opened the door and stormed out. From where he still sat, Zheng pulled a handkerchief from the back pocket of his khaki pants and dabbed his upper lip where a small amount of blood had seeped from the broken vessels in his nose. Having seen Chao's angry rages before, Zheng's personal secretary quietly stood from her desk, hurried over to the door, and shut it so none of the other employees could see her boss recover from another violent run-in with his father.

Swiveling the chair around, Chao stared out over the paradise he'd put his blood, sweat, and tears into. Somehow, some way, he had to ensure he came out of this mess he'd suddenly found himself in without losing everything. "Please, give me strength, oh, great Buddha."

CHAPTER 5

SECONDS AFTER CAMERON EXCUSED HIMSELF FROM the table in the resort's main dining room, Lori glared at her father. "You know, you could at least try to like him and get to know him. He really wanted to make a good impression on you this week, and all you've done is drill him like he's some dweeb who just walked off the bus at basic training."

Avery picked up her glass of wine and took a sip. This was between father and daughter, and she needed to stay out of it, even if she agreed with Lori. The first night at dinner, Brad had interrogated the poor guy, who'd somehow maintained his composure and politeness. Last night hadn't been much better, although Brad had been a little subtler, after Avery's suggestion that he tone it down a little.

Brad rolled his eyes. "I *am* trying to get to know him."

"No, you're not. You're waiting for him to do the slightest thing wrong, so you can tell me he's not good enough. Hell, it's been over forty-eight hours since you've met him, and you're still making him call you 'sir.' He's waiting for you to say 'hey, Cameron, we're on vacation, and I'm not your colonel, so feel free to call me Brad.'" She paused, her facial features softening as she clasped her hands together under her chin. "Dad, please. He means a lot to me."

It was unclear who was more surprised at her use of "Dad" instead of his first name—Lori or Brad —but it seemed to do the trick. He took a deep breath and let it out slowly, staring at his daughter as if really seeing her as a grown woman for the first time. He reached back with one hand and palmed the nape of his neck, rubbing it. "Why do I suddenly get the feeling there's more to this week than just getting to know your new boyfriend?"

As she licked her lips, Lori glanced at Avery, before her gaze found Brad again. "Cameron's starting MARSOC training in three weeks at Camp Lejeune. When he's done and finds out where he's being assigned, I'll be moving there with him."

MARSOC—Marine Corps Forces Special Operations Command—was the Marines' equivalent of the Army's Delta Force and the Navy's SEALs. They were the best of the best and just as badass as their counterparts.

There was a long pause as Lori's words slowly registered in Brad's mind. His eyes narrowed. "Moving there? As in moving *in* with him? Possibly across the country?" She nodded. "And your mother knows about this? Approves of it?"

"Yes, she likes Cam a lot. I'm twenty-four now—most of my friends have moved out of their parents' house and a few have already gotten married. Mom and Richie have their own lives to lead—they want to do a lot more traveling and stuff—and it's time for me to move on and do what feels right. I love Cam. We've already talked about marriage but want to wait until after he's done with his training. Once we know where he's being assigned, I'll check out the shops around there—with my experience, I'll have no trouble finding a job. Eventually, I want to open my own place, but I'll have to build up a new clientele list and reputation there first."

Silence fell over the table as Cameron returned, his confused gaze going from one mute person to the next, clearly trying to figure out what he'd missed but too polite to ask. Crossing his arms, Brad cleared his throat. It seemed as if he'd come to a decision—albeit reluctantly. "Um, Cameron. The . . . uh . . . ladies mentioned earlier they wanted to do some shopping tomorrow. I don't know about you, but that's definitely not my thing."

His back ramrod straight, Cam shook his head once. "Definitely not mine either, sir. I avoid it whenever possible."

"Good. Then why don't you and I go check out those charter boats and see what kind of fish they've been bringing in, hmm? Maybe head out for a few hours and catch a few ourselves."

A genuine smile spread across the younger man's face. "That sounds great, sir."

Brad cleared his throat again and glanced at Avery, who gave him an encouraging dip of her chin. He turned back to Cam. "I think you can knock off the 'sir.' Feel free to call me Brad."

The Marine's eyes widened a bit in surprise. "Thank you, sir . . . I mean, Brad. I appreciate that."

Rolling his lips inward, he nodded. "Okay. Good. Now that that's settled, who's up for dessert?"

The heavy intensity that had been hanging over the table lifted as shoulders relaxed and the conversation changed to lighter topics. While splitting a piece of cheesecake with Lori, the hairs on Avery's neck stood up. Once again, she felt eyes on her. She'd had the same on and off vibes yesterday and today, but she still hadn't located the source. Whoever it was, he or she was good at blending into their surroundings.

Placing her napkin and fork on the table, Avery stood. Brad gave her a probing gaze. "Everything okay?"

She smiled down at him. "Everything's fine. I'm just going to use the ladies' room." When his brow furrowed slightly, she knew he'd heard the mild tension in her tone, but he didn't otherwise acknowledge it. The two of them had worked undercover for years and both were able to appear relaxed and unaffected during times of uncertainty and stress— to most people, that is.

Striding across the dining room, she relied on her acute peripheral vision to study everyone in the room. As she passed the bar, instead of looking at the patrons' backs, she eyed them in the reflection of the mirror that took up most of the wall behind the rows of liquor. The gazes of several people met hers, but there were two men who nabbed her attention. Both were of Asian descent, which, by itself, didn't raise any alarms, but one man's eyes hardened while the other man glanced away quickly, as if he'd been caught looking. They may have just waved a red flag in her face, so maybe they weren't as good as she'd originally thought.

Avery maintained a straight route to her destination—the ladies' room—following two other women in. Whoever the men who'd been watching her were, they were obviously on a surveillance detail, and Avery was positive she was their target. The question was why. Once the door closed behind her, she hurried into a stall and pulled her cell phone out of her small crossbody purse. She quickly typed out a text to Kenny Reardon—geek extraordinaire. He was one of the hackers employed by Deimos with top-secret government clearance. He was also a sweet kid in his midtwenties who she'd come to adore like an adopted son. After Haven had landed in Texas, while recovering from being shot protecting Kenny, he'd asked for a transfer from California to be near her. Since the geek could work behind a computer desk anywhere in the world, it hadn't been a problem. The property Deimos had purchased for Haven to live on, after she'd made the transition from field agent to communications and research tech, had a main house and one small guest cottage that Avery lived in. They'd added on to the latter and made a one-bedroom apartment for Kenny, with a technology setup that would give any computer genius an orgasm just looking at it.

After rereading her text, Avery hit send.

A: Need favor. Hack resort's security feeds. Zero in on bar next to dining room.

Less than five seconds ticked by before she got a response.

K: ?

K: u'r on va-ca

A: Just do it, pls

K: 1 sec

Leaning against the stall's partition, she tapped her nails on the sides of the phone. She knew it wouldn't take long. Before she'd headed over to Brad's house the night before their flight, she'd given Haven and Kenny all the information on her and Brad's flight, car rental, and hotel. Another one of those old habits that wouldn't die.

K: I'm in. What am I looking for?

A: Two Asian men. Closer to lobby. Bttn-down SS shirt on one. Polo on other. Want everything you can find out. Run them thru face recog if u have to.

K: R U ok? Need help?

A: Ok for now. Just get me intel ASAP.

K: Consider it done. I'll get back to u in a bit. Stay safe.

Avery smiled as she typed a final response.

A: k ttyl.

Putting her phone away, she took advantage of where she was, then flushed and left the stall. After washing her hands, she headed back out to the dining room, intent on ignoring the two men, not wanting to give any indication she'd made them. But as she passed where they'd been sitting, the two bar stools were now empty. Glancing around, Avery started to wonder if she'd been wrong about them— was she so out of practice she was seeing danger where there was none?

Reaching the table, she found Brad had already taken care of the bill, and they'd just been waiting for her to return.

"Do you mind if we go meet Tommy and Kiera?" Lori asked, pointing outside the wall of windows overlooking the rest of the resort and the ocean. There was a DJ at the outdoor bar for the evening and many of the younger guests had already gathered.

After glancing at Avery, who gave him a nod, Brad smiled as if he didn't suspect something was wrong. "Sure. You two go on. Avery and I will see you in the morning for breakfast. Have fun."

"Thanks."

After the younger couple waved goodbye, Brad studied Avery's blank face. "Had that feeling again?"

"Yeah. Let's take a walk on the beach." She didn't want to have this conversation in their room. While they took measures to notice if anyone had been in their room, neither one of them had brought a communications jammer. There was the potential for the room being bugged. Once Avery was through filling Brad in on Yin and Yang at the bar, they'd request a different room from the reservations desk.

The night air was warm, but a gentle breeze coming off the water made it comfortable. When they hit the sand, Avery slid her sandals off. Brad took them from her and slung his other arm around her shoulder. No one could ever accuse the some-times-gruff colonel of not being the perfect gentle-man. Avery loved how he did little things like holding out her chair, opening doors, and carrying anything for her that wasn't her purse—although, if it was necessary, she was sure he'd carry that for her too.

They strolled in silence down the beach as small, gentle waves rolled over their feet. When they'd gone a good distance, and Avery was certain they hadn't been followed, she stopped and faced the water. Usually, she hated having her back to any open area, but she trusted Brad to watch her six as he stood in front of her. He could see any threat coming their way, while she could talk low enough that any sound amplifier pointed in her direction would only hear mumbling.

Brad's eyes darted in every direction as Avery explained about the two men at the bar and how she'd contacted Reardon. She took a deep breath and let it out slowly as she glanced up and down the beach, not seeing the two men from the bar nor anyone or anything out of the ordinary. "I've been out of the scene for a long time. Maybe I'm imagining things that aren't there, but my Spidey-senses are screaming at me."

"Then we listen to them," Brad answered in a matter of fact tone. "I'd rather it be a false alarm than something we ignore that turns out to be FUBAR."

Avery agreed—more than once in her career things had been fucked up beyond all recognition— and it was never pretty when it happened. Stepping closer, she wrapped her arms around Brad's waist, reveling in how quickly he hugged her back. While still alert, he smiled down at her. Going up on her tiptoes, she gave him a peck on his lips then settled down again and laid her head against his hard chest. "Have I told you how much it means to me that you and I share the same thought process? Most men I've dated since leaving the field would probably have looked at me like I was crazy if I'd laid all this on them."

His chuckle rumbled against her ear. "It's nice to be with a woman who understands my thought process too. Many times, I was told I was too over-protective and paranoid."

"It's only paranoia if it turns out you're wrong."

Brad squeezed her tightly. "Exactly."

CHAPTER 6

As they strolled back to the hotel, Brad held Avery's hand. Never had he felt such a strong connection to a woman—not even his ex-wife. But Avery got him. She understood what made a man like him tick. Yet, there were still a lot of things he didn't know about her—and vice versa. They'd been dancing around each other for the past few months, neither willing to dive any deeper than they already had. Maybe it was time.

He squeezed her hand. "You know, you never told me why you left the field."

There was a long pause, and he started to wonder if he'd stepped over a line he shouldn't have. But then she let out a deep sigh. "I'd been good at my job. Maybe too good. One day, I'd hit a wall and felt my soul would never find redemption if I continued down the road I was on. The people I'd been ordered to kill . . . their blood is still on my hands. Then there are the people I didn't kill—the ones who got away, whether it was for a few hours, days, or more—the ones who ended up killing others. Innocents who didn't deserve to die. Their blood is on my hands too."

She reached up and tucked a few strands of her hair behind her ear. "I was in a remote part of northern China, tracking a target and waiting for my orders. I was only supposed to gather intel. My cover was that the embassy wanted to help the poor people in that region, and I was there with a team to assess what improvements were needed to help them survive. "The man I was tracking was a ruthless bastard, just like his father. To me, they were the devil and his spawn."

Another couple, out for a moonlight walk, approached them, and Avery paused, waiting until they were out of earshot again. "The family's empire had been built on the backs of others, and they didn't care who they hurt in the process. As long as the money was rolling in, nothing else mattered. Lin Chao, the father, had inherited the legitimate family businesses, but that wasn't enough for him. He got involved in the drug, arms, and slavery trades. He found dirt on every politician and member of law enforcement he could, guaranteeing they were in his back pocket."

Brad knew all about men like that and even a few women. They kept his teams busy trying to take them down and save the innocent. "Sounds all too familiar. China, Colombia, Korea, Russia, Mexico. Hell, there are even some of those bastards in the US. It doesn't matter who they step on in their effort to rule the world, or at least their part of it. So, what happened?"

"The reason Lin Delan and his men were in the area was that they were forging a new route for their arms dealing. His men had terrorized the locals—assaults, rapes, stealing what little they had. One day, in the middle of the village, Delan shot a pregnant woman in the chest at point-blank range because she hadn't moved out of his way fast enough. Just pulled out his gun, shot her, then stepped over her bloody body like she was a mud puddle he was trying to avoid." Her voice had gone cold at the memory, and Brad gave her hand another squeeze, reminding her he was there for her. "One of the men with me was a doctor. Out there, in the middle of nowhere, there wasn't anything he could do to save her, but he could save the baby—she'd been just days away from giving birth. He did a Caesarean, as the life was draining out of her. Mere seconds after hearing her baby boy's cry, she died. Hours later, I got the order to take Delan out. My superiors had found out he and his father had plans to eliminate the US ambassador to China in retaliation for the US's interference in some of their illegal activities. Had it come in earlier, that woman would still be alive, and her child wouldn't have been orphaned."

Brad stopped in front of their resort and pulled her into his arms. He wasn't sure if she was aware she was crying as she made no attempt to wipe away the tears, so he did it for her, cupping her cheeks and using his thumbs. "That's why you went into nursing."

She nodded as best she could with him holding her head. "Mm-hmm. I needed to help save lives. I knew I'd done that with every person I'd killed and every piece of intelligence I'd intercepted, but after taking that bastard down, I was done. I never wanted to take another life again. I called Gene and told him if he didn't pull me out, I'd be a walking time bomb. I was back on US soil within forty-eight hours."

Gene McDaniel had been the head of Deimos

since its inception nearly twenty-five years ago and was well-respected by those who worked for him and the presidents he'd served under. There were very few people he reported to and POTUS was one of them. From what Brad had heard about the man, McDaniel would be holding onto his leadership position until he was either forced out or carried out to the morgue.

"Smart man. I'm sure if you'd made that demand while you were still with the CIA things would have turned out a lot differently."

His hands skimmed down her arms to rest on her hips as Avery cocked her head to the side and smirked. "I'm sure too. But Gene knew I was serious. He also knew I could still be an asset to the agency. When I told him I wanted to leave for good and go into nursing, he was the one who suggested combining the two careers. I've been taking care of injured or sick operatives ever since I became a licensed practical nurse. While about half the states have reciprocity for my certification, the others don't, and I would have had to jump through quite a few hoops to make that happen. Gene took care of all that, so it didn't matter where my patient was located INCONUS."

"Well, I'm just glad Texas was where Haven

ended up because I would have missed out on someone who's become very, very special to me."

Bending down, he brushed his lips against hers. It was there, right on the tip of his tongue, to tell her exactly how he felt about her. Was this the right time? He'd never thought he'd get remarried, but now he couldn't help wondering what it would be like to stand before their family and friends, with Avery in a beautiful, white dress, as they professed their undying love for each other. Or maybe they'd elope, and it would just be the two of them. Either way, he would love to grow old with her by his side.

He gazed into her eyes and suddenly he knew. Avery felt the same way about him, but she was scared and uncertain. She'd gotten to this point in her life without ever marrying. Hell, as far as he could tell, there'd never been someone special, long term, in her life—someone who had cherished her no matter what came their way. How the men who'd crossed her path over the years had never tried to snatch her up permanently, he'd never understand, but their loss was his gain. While she wasn't ready to hear his intent to someday put a ring on her finger— yup, Bradley Barton was officially off the market— he could at least start things moving in that direction.

With the moon and stars high above them and the ocean lapping against the shoreline, Brad prepared to say the three words he'd only said to one other woman who hadn't been a blood relative. He was certain he'd never say them to any other woman ever again. Taking her hands in his, he brought them to his mouth and kissed her knuckles as he stared into her eyes, letting her see all the emotion welling up inside of him. "Avery, I love you."

Tears filled her eyes as her jaw dropped. It took her a moment to gather herself before she threw her arms around his neck and held him tightly. "Oh, thank God! I've wanted to say that for weeks now, but I was so scared you didn't feel the same."

A grin spread across Brad's face as he chuckled then leaned back so he could see her. "I think that means you love me too, right?" He desperately needed to hear the words.

"Yes! Yes, I love you, Shrek." She went up on her toes and melded her lips to his. Never in his life had something felt so damn right.

CHAPTER 7

"I don't know about you, but I'm all shopped out," Lori said, holding up the multiple bags that were weighing down her arms.

They'd spent the past three hours roaming the huge, crowded street market in town, with over a hundred vendors hawking everything a tourist could want, along with a ton of stuff they didn't need. While Avery had picked up a few things along the way, she hadn't really been into the whole excursion. That feeling of being watched had been with her since they'd left the resort, but she hadn't seen either of the men from the bar last night, nor anyone else tailing her, for that matter. So far, whoever these assholes were, they'd only been doing reconnaissance. The intel she'd gotten from Kenny this morning hadn't helped her figure out why she was being targeted. Liang Guo and Feng Su, both in their early twenties, were local petty criminals who'd been arrested for fights, possession of drugs, picking pockets, etc. Liang had emigrated from China about six years ago while Feng had been born to his immigrant parents on the island. Other than that, there'd been little else of importance in their histories. If last night had been the only incident where she'd felt like she was being watched, Avery might have written off the two men's actions as simply sizing up the tourists, so they could rip them off somehow.

Avery hadn't been surprised when Haven had called a few minutes after Kenny had hung up with a promise to keep looking into Liang and Feng. Having already been filled in by the geek the night before, the younger, female Deimos agent had wanted all the details she was missing—which weren't many. Then, before disconnecting the call, Haven told Avery to expect a knock on their hotel room door in exactly twenty minutes and to not bother with a tip—it'd all been taken care of. When Brad had opened the door, a nondescript kid around the age of eighteen or nineteen silently handed him a large, black duffel bag before scurrying toward the stairwell instead of the elevator. Brad eyed both ends of the hallway then ducked back into the new room they'd moved into the night before, locking the door behind him. Setting the duffel on the bed, he'd unloaded the cache of weapons and equipment, not the least bit stunned at how quickly Haven had arranged things. While they hadn't left the room since moving into it, Brad had still used a bug detector to ensure there were no listening or video devices hidden in the room. He'd then set up a jammer that would prevent their cell phone calls from being intercepted, followed by several motion-sensor cameras that would send an alert to both their phones if anyone entered the room while they were out.

Now, as she walked side by side with Lori, Avery felt a lot more comfortable with the compact Sig Sauer pistol tucked in the waistband of her shorts at the small of her back. A stiletto knife was under the back strap of her bra, while a switchblade was sitting snugly under her breasts. She and Brad had discussed staying at the resort, but neither had wanted to disappoint Lori and Cameron—well, Brad hadn't wanted to disappoint Lori. They also hadn't wanted to try to explain a bunch of weird suspicions. As far as Lori and Cam knew, Avery had been a nurse her whole adult life. They knew nothing of her black-ops years or the number of people who'd died at her hand. While she and Lori had walked around, Avery had taken all precautions to make sure they remained surrounded by plenty of people, plus she didn't know if the possible threat was due to her past or if it was just a coincidence—something she didn't truly believe in. Hell, she didn't even know if she was the target or if it was Brad, Lori, or Cam. As long as Avery stayed alert, things would be okay. Still, she was glad to hear Lori was ready to head back to the resort.

"Sounds good to me," she said to the younger woman. "I think I hear a Mai Tai calling my name."

Lori smiled. "I *know* a piña colada is calling mine." Her eyes lit up at something over Avery's shoulder. "Oh, here comes a taxi; let's grab it."

A bright, yellow minivan pulled up to the curb not far from them and let two touristy-looking men out. When they walked in the opposite direction from the women, not even giving them a glance, Avery's tensed shoulders relaxed again. The men from the bar last night were nowhere in sight, nor did anyone else seem out of place or overly interested in the two female tourists. That still didn't make Avery feel any better. Even after years of not being in the field, it was difficult for her not to suspect every single person within a mile radius of being a bad guy.

Keeping an eye on their surroundings, Avery followed Lori, who quickly spoke to the dark-skinned driver through the front passenger window, giving him the name of their resort. When he responded with the same fare amount as it had cost them to get there, Lori opened the rear sliding door and jumped in. Out of habit, Avery checked the bench seat and floor behind the middle seat before climbing in and shutting the door. They could have taken the rental car, but the concierge at the resort had advised them to take a taxi since parking was chaotic and overpriced in the area around the market. After seeing it for themselves when they'd first arrived, Avery had been glad they'd listened to the man.

"Hello, beautiful ladies," the driver said with a huge grin, showing off several missing teeth. As soon as they were settled in their seats, he pulled away from the curb and maneuvered into the local traffic. "I see you enjoyed the market today."

"Yes, we did," Lori agreed. "I don't know how I'm going to get all of this home in my suitcase though."

"A lot of tourists have that problem."

As the two chatted amicably, Avery turned sideways in her seat, facing Lori, so she could inspect the vehicles behind them to see if they were being followed. By the time they'd left the busy streets surrounding the market and moved onto the quieter main road that lead to their resort, Avery was almost convinced they didn't have a tail. But then a white van appeared behind them, speeding to catch up. Avery tensed. Her hand settled on the gun at her lower back, ready to draw and fire if need be.

Their driver noticed the vehicle in the rearview mirror and turned the steering wheel enough so they hugged the dirt shoulder of the road yet maintained the speed limit. He didn't seem concerned. "Some people are always in a hurry. Don't they know we're on island time?"

The vehicle never slowed down as it veered around them and kept going, disappearing around a curve. Avery released the weapon and forced herself to relax. Jeez, this was supposed to be a stress-free vacation. Well, at least her relationship with Brad was progressing better than she'd hoped for. She'd been so worried when she'd realized she was head over heels in love with him. For the first time in her life, she wanted a future with a man more than she wanted her next breath. There'd been other men in her life, but none of them had had her dreaming of growing old with them. They'd been a fun way to pass the time, and, when the relationships were over, she'd moved on without any regrets. Now, she was glad none of those affairs had worked out because they'd led her to Brad. The man she loved. The man who loved her. The man she wanted to spend the rest of her life with.

A short curse from the front seat preceded the driver slamming on the brakes. Tires screeched as Avery and Lori, unrestrained, were thrown against the backs of the front seats. Avery's head and shoulder exploded with pain as the vehicle spun around, sending her crashing against the door and smashing the window into tiny pieces. She had no clue what had caused the driver to lose control, she just hoped they survived the accident. Lori screamed in pain as the two were tossed around the back seat. The taxi went off the road, coming to an abrupt stop when it collided with a tree.

The loud chaos ebbed until a quiet stillness took over. Avery's head spun. Every inch of her body was in pain, but, as she'd learned long ago, that was good because it meant she was still alive. She slowly pushed herself upright. Lori was wedged between the bench seat and the back of the driver's seat, her shoulder at an unnatural angle. Blood flowed from a cut along her hairline, but she was conscious and groaning. Their driver, however, was not. The man was slumped over the steering wheel. Avery reached over to help Lori, but suddenly hands were grabbing her and pulling her out the destroyed window. Her gold necklace got caught on something and snapped from her neck. She struggled, but the trauma her body had endured had sapped her strength. Her stomach threatened to revolt as her head swam, darkness trying to overtake her. She was being carried with no care for her injuries. She heard a sliding door and was dropped unceremoniously into the rear of a van. A pain-filled cry escaped her. Seconds later, Lori was thrown in beside her, along with all their shopping bags. The door slammed shut, and the van started rolling, then accelerated to a high rate of speed. Avery fought unconsciousness, but the bastard won as her world went black.

CHAPTER 8

BRAD COULDN'T BELIEVE HE WAS SMILING AS HE AND
Cameron strode down the dock. It'd actually been a
good day hanging out and fishing with his daughter's boyfriend. Maybe it was because Brad had been
so relaxed after the night he'd spent making love to
Avery. Admitting you were in love with a woman,
really in love, made for some amazing sex—not that
they'd had any trouble in that department before.

"That was a helluva fish you brought up, Brad,"
Cameron said. "Damn thing put up a good fight."

"Not bad for an old man, right?"

The younger man's mouth flapped a few times.
"Th-That's not what I meant, sir."

Brad raised an eyebrow at him. "What? The
Marines didn't teach you how to take a joke?" The

relief that crossed Cameron's face was enough to make Brad laugh.

"Ha! All right, you got me."

Reaching the end of the dock, they turned right to head back to the resort, which was only a short distance away. Brad stuck his hands into the pockets of his cargo shorts. The 9mm subcompact, with the filed off serial number, in the back of his waistband felt reassuring despite it being illegal. Like most men and women in the military and law enforcement, he felt naked when not armed. "So . . . what made you choose the Marines?"

Cameron glanced at him as if the question had caught him off guard. They'd met three middle-aged men from Florida on board the boat and had spent most of the trip conversing with them, in between catching a bunch of fish, so Brad hadn't asked Cameron many personal questions. But sometime during the trip he'd found himself joking and laughing with the young Marine—and liking him. It was as if once his daughter had been removed from the equation, the two men had ended up on equal footing, even with an almost-thirty-year gap between them.

Brad wasn't thrilled the guy was sleeping with Lori—well, he didn't know that for sure, but Avery was probably right, and they were consenting adults —but his daughter could've done far worse when choosing a boyfriend. Cameron reminded Brad of the Deltas under his command, after they'd finished their special-ops training and joined the ranks of an elite brotherhood of men who'd lay down their lives for each other and innocent people they'd never met. He was pretty sure Cameron would survive the intense MARSOC course and become a Marine Raider. At least the kid would never be under Brad's command, so he guessed it was a good thing they were in different branches of the military.

"My dad was a Marine. He was KIA in Desert Storm while my mom was pregnant with me."

Brad's mouth flattened. "Sorry to hear that, son. I lost quite a few friends over there myself." He'd been several ranks lower during the Gulf War and a green Delta, fresh out of the intensive, six-month OTC— Operator Training Course. His first mission overseas had earned him his first Bronze Star and Purple Heart. Several other members of his team had earned them as well. The mission hadn't been pretty, but they'd all survived. He couldn't say the same for several missions that'd followed.

They walked in a heavy silence for a few moments before Cameron spoke again. "My mom wasn't thrilled when I told her I wanted to enlist instead of going to college, but she understood I wanted to honor the man who gave me life and gave his own, so I could live free. My father had put in a request for Force Recon a month before he was killed. I wanted to do what he never had the chance to." Many of the USMC Force Recon units had been integrated into MARSOC after it was formed in 2005.

"I'm sure he would have been proud of the man you've become."

A sad smile spread appeared on Cameron's face. "Thanks. I like to think so."

Brad reached up and placed his hand on the younger man's shoulder, stopping him short. "And you're the kind of man my daughter deserves. You have honor and integrity, and you make her happy. That's all I want for her."

His eyes grew wide. "Thank you, that means a lot to me."

"You're welcome." Brad started them walking again. "Just don't fuck up and hurt her because they'll never find your body."

Cameron laughed as the melancholy mood that had settled around them lifted again. "Yes, sir. Understood."

They reached the entrance to the resort, and Brad nodded at a man who exited and held the door open for them. "Thank you." He then turned to Cameron. "C'mon. Let's go find our women and a few beers."

"Sounds good to me."

Ten minutes later, the two ended up in the lobby again after failing to find the women in their rooms, out by the pool, or anywhere else in the resort. Brad pulled out his cell phone and called Avery, leaving a message when it went to voice mail. "Hi, baby. I know you're not a big shopper so that means my daughter is doing some serious damage to her credit cards if you're still at the market. Give me a call when you're on your way back. Cameron and I will be at the bar by the pool. Love you." He disconnected the call and pointed at the younger man. "First beer's on you."

Striding back out to the bar that overlooked the pool and ocean, Brad's eyes narrowed when he spotted a couple sitting at one of the tables. The dark-haired beauty was wearing sunglasses and a pink bikini that had the human dogs around her slobbering despite the man sitting next to her—a man they didn't want to fuck with. He was tall, lean, and in peak physical condition, a fact that couldn't be hidden by the T-shirt and cargo shorts he was wearing. His long, blond hair was pulled back and tied at his nape, and his eyes, which Brad knew were blue, were covered by dark sunglasses. What made him dangerous was the fact he probably knew well over two dozen ways to kill someone—so did his woman. Luckily for Brad, the two were on Uncle Sam's side. T. Carter and Jordyn Alvarez were Deimos operatives. In other words, they were both spies and assassins for the US. Jordyn was good friends with Haven and Avery, and she and Carter had also been on the mission when Haven had been shot in the back, effectively ending her career as a field agent. The couple had stood by her during her long recovery, which is how Brad had met and gotten to know them. The question was, though, what were they doing at his resort in Aruba?

Smiling, Carter held up his beer to the newcomers as they approached. "Barton, my good man. Fancy running into you here. Pull up a chair. This must be your daughter's boyfriend. The fact he hasn't been dumped out in the middle of the ocean impresses me."

Jordyn chuckled. "That's a good thing, Cameron. It takes a lot to impress him, trust me."

His eyebrows shot up at his name being spoken,

and Brad was certain that wasn't the only intel the woman had gotten from Haven. She'd surely given all the information she'd gathered when Brad had asked her to do a background check on the younger man after finding out his last name. Brad could have gone through Ghost or one of his other operatives, but he preferred to keep his professional life separate from his personal one—at least, as best he could. While she hadn't given him many details, Haven had assured him his daughter's boyfriend appeared to be an upstanding guy, and Brad should just chill and get to know him the way most fathers would.

Cameron stared at Jordyn. "Well, since I don't know you, it's kind of hard for me to trust you at the moment." His tone was polite despite his wariness. The man had good instincts and responses, which would serve him well in special ops. His gaze went to Brad. "Friends of yours?"

"You could say that." He pulled out one of the empty chairs at the table and sat, indicating for the Marine to do the same. "T. Carter, Jordyn Alvarez, as you've obviously learned, this is Cameron McGee." He gave the younger man a reassuring nod. "Avery mentioned you and Lori when she was talking to Haven last night on the phone. Carter and Jordyn work with Haven." As far as Lori and Cameron knew, Avery was exactly as she appeared to be—a long-term-duty nurse, helping a US-government employee recover from a spinal injury. Haven, they'd been told, had been injured in a car accident while in China where she'd been working as a translator for the US embassy. Now, she lived in Texas while still translating documents and doing research for the government.

A curvaceous waitress in a black sarong and bikini top stopped at their table. "Can I get you anything, gentlemen?" she practically purred.

Her very-interested gaze blatantly flitted from one man to the next, lingering on Carter and ignoring Jordyn, who growled and pulled off her sunglasses, revealing her blazing, chocolate eyes. "As long as it comes out of a bottle, sweetheart, and I'm not talking about the bleach you use on your hair. Trust me, you'll earn a bigger tip if you stop drooling over my man."

Carter dipped his chin down, trying to hide his amused grin, as the waitress's jaw dropped. Brad and Cameron quickly ordered a beer each, and Carter raised his, silently indicating he'd take another Corona with lime. When the bleached blonde scurried away, Jordyn tossed her sunglasses onto the table as she glared daggers at the woman's retreating back. Carter's shoulders started to shake as he snickered. "Jealous much, baby?"

"What? That's the third time she ignored me in the last half hour, and I'll be damned if I'm going to sit here and watch her salivate over you." Mournfully, she looked at the half-finished strawberry daiquiri on the table in front of her. "But I guess that means I can't order another one of these. She'll probably spit in it. Damn."

Reaching over, Carter brushed his thumb along her jaw. "I'll go to the bar and get you another when you're ready for it."

Her facial features softened as she leaned into his touch. "Thank you."

"My pleasure."

Brad leaned forward and rested his forearms on the table. "Now that that's taken care of, want to tell me what you're doing here?"

Carter shrugged and then relaxed back in his chair as if he didn't have a care in the world, but that didn't mean he wasn't one-hundred percent aware of their surroundings. He could probably rattle off astute observations he'd made about every person around them, having analyzed everyone's threat potential within minutes of arriving. "We were visiting friends on Caicos and had a few more days off. Haven mentioned you and Avery were here, so we decided to take the ninety-minute flight to say hi. It's been a while since we visited Aruba, and it's one of Jordy's favorite islands."

That big lie was for Cameron's benefit. Brad didn't question the "friends on Caicos," because he'd heard them mention knowing people on the small Caribbean island before—a couple named Jase and Brie. That had probably been the truth. That it was one of Ms. Alvarez's favorite islands might also be true. The stopping by and saying "hi" had been the lie. These two people didn't just show up out of the blue without a reason. Haven had to have told them about Avery and Brad's suspicions someone had been following them, and she'd sent them as backup. Well, when it came to his woman and his daughter, Brad wasn't too proud to ask for help. Having the two spies watching their six made him feel a lot better. He also didn't doubt they came by private jet, ensuring they could bring some serious fire power with them. There would be no kid dropping off a loaded, black duffel bag.

"Well, then, glad you could join us. You manage to get a room here?"

"Yes," Jordyn responded. "We're on the third

floor." It didn't surprise Brad they were on the same floor as him and Avery. Lori and Cameron had the room across the hall from them, and it was a sure bet Jordyn and Carter now occupied one of the four rooms next to either of those two. "Where are Avery and Lori?"

"Out shopping at some huge market; they should be back soon." But twenty minutes later, with still no sign of the two women, nor a call from them, the four of them started to get concerned. Brad had called Avery's phone again, while Cameron had tried to reach Lori. Both calls had gone to voice mail.

Carter set his beer down. "Brad, why don't you take the kid here, and we'll follow you to the market and see if we can find them. Leave word at the concierge for them to call you if Avery and Lori show up."

As they all stood, Brad nodded. "Yeah, but I think we need to get Cameron some gear first. You have extra?"

"Of course," Carter answered with an eye roll, as if it'd been an inane question in the first place.

Cameron's eyes narrowed. "What do you mean?"

Cocking his head toward the hotel, Brad said, "We'll explain upstairs."

When they reached the spies' room, Jordyn

grabbed some clothes and ducked into the bathroom, closing the door behind her. Meanwhile, Brad told Cameron about Avery's suspicions that someone had been tailing her. "We haven't been approached by anyone, and aside from the two men at the bar last night, no one else has raised a red flag. Avery's carrying and is former black-ops—it's the only reason I let them out of my sight today."

Carter then gave Cameron a very abbreviated version of who he and Jordyn really were, along with a loaded Smith & Wesson 9mm with two spare clips and a holster. "All you need to know, kid, is we're the good guys, with more US-government clearance than you'll ever know, even after you end up in special-ops." Yup, Haven had definitely passed on a lot of intel about Cameron.

Taking the weapon, the young Marine checked the clip and chamber to make sure they were loaded. He then holstered it at his lower back and put the spare clips in the cargo pocket on the side of his thigh. "And if I ever mention your name after this I'll end up six-feet under somewhere and they'll never find my body, right?"

Despite the seriousness of the situation, Carter grinned broadly. "Something like that." He looked at Brad and cocked his head back toward Cameron. "I like him. He'd fit in well with the Trident boys. You know how Ian loves sarcasm."

Brad snorted. "Ian is the definition of the word. I wouldn't be surprised to see his photo next to it in the dictionary."

"True that."

The door to the bathroom swung open again, and Jordyn walked out dressed in a pair of multi-pocketed capri pants and a loose shirt that would hide any weapons on her body. As she loaded up with several firearms and knives, Carter handed Brad a legal gun, which he placed at the small of his back. He then strapped a holster to his ankle and stuck the gun Haven had had delivered into it. Since it was a weapon with a questionable background, it was best he didn't use it, but it still might come in handy later. He didn't want to think about why. For now, there was a more important matter at hand— finding his woman and daughter.

CHAPTER 9

His heart pounding, Brad pulled the keys out of his pocket as he and Cameron jogged toward the rental car. Jordyn and Carter were heading toward a tan SUV a few spaces down. They'd gotten directions to the market from the concierge. It was about a ten-minute drive down a winding road into the main town and then a few blocks over from there. Brad prayed the women hadn't gotten into trouble and would be passing them along the way. He knew they'd gotten there okay several hours earlier because Avery had sent him a text, with two photos, asking what color he preferred for a shirt she'd wanted to get him. He'd gotten a warm feeling in his chest as he'd typed in an answer to her. It had been a long time since a woman had bought him something with his input. Some women had gifted him with clothes, but most of the time it'd been something he'd never pick out for himself, much less wear, but Avery had found a shirt that was definitely his style. Damn, he loved that woman.

After a little over two miles, they came around a curve and Brad slowed the vehicle to a stop. There was a police car and a tow truck idling on the side of the road with their lights flashing. A heavy winch was dragging a demolished taxi up a small incline at the side of the road, where it had apparently hit a tree. Pulling onto the opposite shoulder, Brad left the car running as he jumped out with Cameron following. Jordyn and Carter joined them as they approached the police officer and tow truck driver.

Brad addressed the cop. "Excuse me. Can you tell me if two women were in there?"

The uniformed man shook his head. "Only person in there was a male driver. He's on his way to the hospital in critical condition."

"Was he thrown out of the vehicle?" Carter asked as he eyed the missing rear passenger window on the driver's side of the mini-van, as the tow truck operator made some adjustments to the winch.

"No. He was found in the driver's seat."

"Then whose blood is this?" He pointed to

several drops and smears of red on the window frame.

"There's blood on this window too," Jordyn announced from the other side as she slid open the door to inspect the back seat.

The cop shook his head again, this time in confusion. "I have no idea. The driver was the only occupant. Witnesses who came upon the accident shortly after it happened never mentioned seeing any passengers. The blood must be from when the paramedics were taking him out."

"How long ago did the accident happen?" Brad asked, his panic rising.

"About a half hour ago."

Jordyn came back around holding something in her closed hand. She furtively gestured to Brad, Carter, and Cameron to head back to where their vehicles waited for them on the other side of the road. When they were out of the cop's earshot, Jordyn opened her fist, and Brad's heart clenched when he saw what she was holding. It was a gold necklace with a charm on it. He knew without looking closer it was a St. Agatha medal—the patron saint of nurses. Avery and her friend, Judi, had gotten matching ones after graduating from nursing school. Avery rarely took hers off.

Swallowing hard, fear coursing through him, he held out his hand, and Jordyn placed the delicate piece of jewelry in it as Carter pulled out his cell phone and hit a speed dial button. When the call connected, he said, "Haven, it's Carter. I need you to ping Avery's phone. If there's no response, activate her tracker."

Shit. Brad had forgotten all about that. Apparently, all Deimos operatives and support staff had a small implant that'd been inserted under their skin near their shoulder blades in case they went missing. The device would be activated only in emergencies or if someone went rogue. Avery's was still in place, even though she was no longer an agent.

As Jordyn whipped out her phone and began to make a call, most likely to Gene McDaniel, their boss, Brad's own phone rang. His hope that it was Avery calling died quickly when he saw the name on the screen. Swiping the screen, he answered the call. "Barton."

"What's going on, Colonel?" Frisco asked. Evidently, he was in the same room as his fiancée.

"Avery and Lori took a taxi into town to shop at an outdoor market a few hours ago. When they didn't come back, and we couldn't get them on their phones, we headed toward the market to search for them. We came upon an accident involving a taxi. There's evidence there were more occupants than just the driver, but no one knows who they were or where they went, but it had to be Avery and Lori. Jordyn found Avery's St. Agatha medal in the back seat."

"Shit. Do you want me to call the base and get a team down there?"

Brad's mind was ready to explode. As much as he wanted to call in every Delta operative under his command, he couldn't. Using military personnel for personal reasons was broadly frowned upon and could get him in a ton of trouble with his superiors —especially since they weren't on US soil. He also hoped they found Avery and Lori long before the Deltas could get boots on the island. He eyed the two Deimos spies and Cameron. He knew, just like him, they'd move heaven and earth to find the two women, and God help anyone who got in their way.

"No. Hold off on that for now. We have to figure out what we're dealing with first."

"Understood, sir. Should I at least call Colonel Sheppard, Captain Bryson, and Captain Nielsen and give them a head's up?" Frisco's and Ghost's teams were the only two currently stateside. The third team under Brad's command was currently on the other side of the world, being monitored by Sheppard in Texas.

Dragging a hand down his face, the coarse, days-old facial hair rasping against his palm, Brad tried to focus. It was Carter's spat curse behind him that spurred him into action again. "Yeah, tell them." Without another word, he disconnected the call, knowing his subordinate wouldn't be offended, and even if he was, it didn't matter. All that *did* matter now was getting Avery and Lori back. He turned to face the spy, hoping whatever bad news he'd gotten was something they could work around.

"Keep trying," Carter said to Haven. "Call me as soon as you have anything." He hung up the phone. "It pinged once on the north end of the island before it disappeared. There's a glitch in the satellite; the techs at HQ are trying to unscramble it. All we have is a general area."

After disconnecting her call, Jordyn rejoined them. "Gene's trying to find some nearby help, but it might take them more than a few hours to get here. It depends on how fast he can get ahold of them." She eyed Carter. "Jase and additional gear are a phone call and ninety minutes away. Two hours with land travel time."

"I was thinking the same thing. We've got time to

kill until we get more intel." The spy pulled out his phone again, dialed, and waited a moment for the call to connect. "A-man, your services are needed. Tell me you've got access to a plane and can get to Aruba, locked and loaded, in under two hours; it's an emergency." He paused. "Awesome. Get me on the phone when you land, and I'll give you a rendezvous point." He didn't put the phone away, instead, made another call. "Reardon, Avery and . . . of course, Haven already called you. Get that artificial intelligence of yours running through the list of residents on Aruba. Start with the passports, and if nothing hits, move onto the airline manifests for the past two weeks, local driver's licenses, and arrest records, in that order . . . I know the population is just over 100,000 people without the damn tourists—just do it. She didn't have the feeling of being watched until they landed on the island, so my guess is whoever it is was already here. I want to know if any names crossmatch with Avery's past missions . . . Don't worry; we'll find them . . . Yeah, good."

"What now?" Cameron asked after Carter ended the call. "Are we calling in the cops or doing this ourselves?"

Brad studied the two spies for a moment before answering. "We're on our own, for now. If this has something to do with Avery's past, which is a big possibility, the cops will just fuck it up. Hell, it'll take too long to convince them there's something more going on than two tourists who lost track of time."

"I agree." Carter nodded as he glanced at the phone in his hand after it chirped with an incoming text. "Haven's arms contact is agreeing to meet us with some more firepower and gear. Let's go."

CHAPTER 10

"AVERY, WAKE UP. PLEASE, PLEASE, WAKE UP."

Lori's insistent, anguished whispering filtered into Avery's scrambled mind, but it was quickly shoved out again by the pain coursing through her body. Everything hurt—and that was an understatement. She'd been injured before—broken bones and a few wounds needing stitches—but with a normally high tolerance for pain, never had the word "agony" been something she could physically relate to. Until now. *Shit.*

She blinked her eyes and had a moment of panic when everything remained pitch dark. Was she blind? She gently moved her head to the side. *Oh, thank God.* There was a small sliver of light coming from under a closed door. Unfortunately, it didn't illuminate much beyond an inch or two into the room. Movement from her left told her where Lori was, and Avery reached out to touch her, finding her thigh and causing the young woman to gasp with relief. Avery squeezed Lori's leg. "I'm here, wherever *here* is. Are you okay?"

"I—I think so, but my shoulder's dislocated, and I have a cut on my forehead that was bleeding. I think it's stopped, or at least slowed, but I can't get my damn shoulder back in. It's popped out before, and I've always had to go to the ER to get it put back in." Although Avery couldn't see the younger woman, it sounded like she was gritting her teeth from the pain. "Where are we and why? Who were those men that took us?"

Those were the million-dollar questions. Too bad she didn't have the answers—yet.

"I don't know. Hell, I don't even know what caused the accident."

"As we came around the curve, that van that'd passed us was stopped, blocking the road. Our driver slammed on the brakes and lost control. Next thing I knew, we were being yanked out of the taxi."

Avery had a vague recollection of being pulled through the taxi's window, not that it mattered now.

"Did you lose consciousness at any point? Any idea if we're still in Aruba?"

"Yeah, we are. They drove about . . . I don't know . . . twenty minutes, maybe longer. It was hard to tell. They handcuffed us to a bar in the van, then put hoods over our heads. When we got here, they didn't take the hoods off until they'd moved us into this room. I barely got a look at it before they shut the door, and everything went dark. That was maybe ten or fifteen minutes ago. Like I said, it's hard to tell."

Pushing herself up into a sitting position, Avery took stock of her own injuries. She probably had a concussion since her head felt like it was split open down the center—having lost consciousness for a while wasn't good either. She had some cuts and bruises, all which appeared to be non-life-threatening, but nothing seemed to be broken. She quickly became aware of the fact that the gun was gone from her lower back. A check of the front and back of her bra revealed that those weapons had been found and removed as well. Whoever their captors were, they were thorough.

"Which shoulder, Lori?" Avery asked as she unclasped her bra from beneath her shirt and pulled it out from the sleeves in a move practically every woman alive knew how to do.

"My left."

As gently as she could, Avery used her hands to figure out how Lori was positioned. "I can probably pop it back in, but it's going to hurt like a bitch."

"Been there, done that, got the T-shirt. I know it'll hurt, but once it's back in it will hurt far less than it does now. How are you going to pop it in, though?"

"I'm going to put my bra under your armpit, then yank upward while using my foot to push down on your clavicle. It's the best I can do under the circumstances. Think you can handle it?"

"Can I cuss like a sailor while you're doing it?"

"Sure." The corners of Avery's mouth ticked upward despite the situation. Brad may not have been in the same state as his daughter for much of her life, but she'd definitely inherited his strength and grit. Maybe a few screams and curses would bring someone running, and Avery could get some answers—not that she was looking forward to hurting the other woman. "Hang tight for a minute. Let me make sure we have enough room."

"Okay. I haven't been able to move far with my shoulder like this, but I didn't hit anything except the wall behind me and another to my left. I guess that doesn't really help you, though, since you can't see which direction that is."

After getting to her knees, Avery blindly felt around. She didn't know if anything or anyone else was in there with them. The concrete floor was rough and dirty. So were the four walls. The door was steel and locked from the outside, but it hadn't been expertly hung since light emanated from the bottom and lower half of one side. By the time she'd circumnavigated the whole room, she guessed it was approximately twelve foot square. Aside from Lori and Avery, the walls, one door, the floor, and, presumably, a ceiling, the only other thing in there with them was warm, muggy air, which was to be expected on an island.

Once she knew she had enough space to work in, she inched her way back to Lori, and found her foot. Since the injury was on her left side, Avery worked her way up the younger woman's right until she was behind her. "Swivel to your right a little and then lie on your back as best as you can. I'll support your back as you ease down."

"Okay . . . Oh, fuck, shit, damn, motherfucker!" Lori barked between growls as she got into position. By the time she was supine on the floor, she was panting from the pain. "Arrrghhh! Shit! Hurry!"

Carefully, Avery felt her way down Lori's head, face, and chest, trying to avoid touching her arm or shoulder until she had too. "This is where it's gonna start hurting—well, worse than it is. Take a deep breath."

When she heard the ragged intake of air, followed by a second, she threaded her bra under Lori's forearm, then shimmied the two ends of the garment upward until it was snug in her armpit. Muttered curses and gasps came from Lori's mouth, but she was doing pretty well, considering. Sitting down, Avery brought her right knee to her chest and laid her left leg alongside Lori's injured arm. She set her right foot on top of Lori's shoulder, as close to her neck as possible, and wrapped both ends of her bra around her hands to make sure she didn't lose them in the process. "All right, Lori. Here we go. I'm going to push down with my foot and pull up hard on your shoulder."

"Just do it!"

Avery shoved down with her foot and yanked with her arms in one combined motion. Lori shrieked as her shoulder moved and popped back into place. Letting go of the bra, Avery never had a chance to ask the other woman if she was okay, because the door flew open, slamming against the wall, bright light filtering in, temporarily blinding them. A bald, Asian man, standing about six foot three, with broad shoulders and a semi-automatic in his hand, shouted at them in Chinese. Although it had been a few years since she'd last had a conversation, beyond a sentence or two, in the Mandarin dialect, she understood the curses and demand to know what the fuck was going on. She responded in the same language, uncertain if the man knew any English. "She's injured," she stated, as if that explained everything, but the resulting expression on the man's face told her he didn't care. "Where are we? Why are we here? Who's in charge?"

"That would be me," another voice said in Mandarin, as a man from her past rounded the door jamb.

Avery's eyes and nostrils flared. *Oh, shit on a stick. This isn't good.*

"Hello, Ms. McNamara. I never thought I'd say this, but it's a pleasure to see you again." His sneer said otherwise. It'd been over a decade since anyone had called her by her undercover name. It felt so surreal to hear it now. She'd met Lin Chao at several political functions during her time in China. Even if she hadn't already known what an evil person he was, at the time, she still wouldn't have liked the man. He was one of those narcissistic bastards who thought all women were beneath him unless they were on top, fucking or sucking him.

Standing, she channeled her old persona, her back straightening in defiance. The last person she'd ever expected to walk through the door was the father of the man she'd assassinated on her last op. Lin Chao and his eldest son had been on Deimos's watch list in the months leading up to the moment Avery had ended the younger man's life. Even though both men had been cunning and smart, Delan had had a cruel streak with even loftier aspirations than his father. The US government had learned Delan had been making connections within several Middle Eastern facets—including Al Qaeda and ISIS, the latter still in its infancy but growing quickly. Where Chao had been greedy, Delan had been greedy *and* deadly. His affiliation with known terrorist groups made him a threat to American troops and citizens and had sealed his fate. "Lin Chao. Well, well, well. I thought you were exiled to the South Pole."

"Bitch." He backhanded Avery, knocking her to the floor as Lori, who was still sitting, gasped.

Yeah, it probably hadn't been a smart thing to antagonize the man. Despite the pain exploding throughout her face and head again, Avery got to her feet and put herself between Lori and Chao. So far, the latter hadn't even acknowledged the other woman's presence beyond a dismissive glance, and Avery wanted to keep it that way. She had to keep them both alive long enough for Brad to realize they were missing. Once that happened, he was sure to call Haven, who would know to activate the tracking device in Avery's shoulder. She'd never been so happy for the tiny piece of technology that had been embedded under her skin. It'd been years since she'd thought about the foreign object she prayed was still operational.

"You'll pay for your crimes. You'll suffer until you beg for your death. Then you'll suffer more until I finally grant your wish." Chao snapped his fingers. "Take her to the other room."

The tall, bald man stepped forward and snatched Avery's upper arm, pulling her toward the door as if she weighed nothing, while Lori struggled to her feet. Tears rolled down her cheeks. Her loud voice was tinged with confusion and fear. "No! Leave her alone! Why are you doing this?"

Chao switched to English. "Shut up, and I may let you live. This doesn't concern you, but I have no qualms about disposing of you along with this murdering cunt."

He turned on his heel and followed his minion and Avery out the door. Glancing over her shoulder and seeing the disbelief and terror on Lori's face, Avery raised her voice as she was dragged around the corner of the door jamb. "Lori, do everything they tell you! Stay strong! Don't give them any reason to hurt you! It'll be okay!" As she was led to God knew where, she prayed they'd both get out of this alive.

CHAPTER 11

"Jase, this is Brad and Cameron," Carter said, keeping the introduction brief in his three-room suite at the resort. "It's their women who are missing."

Over the past two hours, they hadn't learned anything more, but did change their minds about filing a missing person's report on both women. As expected, though, the local cops weren't much help. While Brad and Jordyn were able to convince the detective they spoke to that Avery and Lori had been in the wrecked taxi, the man's hands were tied without any witnesses. The driver was still unconscious at the hospital and the detective would interview him if he woke up. Other than that, the cops were currently useless to Brad.

Cameron stepped forward and held out his hand. "Thanks for coming."

"You're welcome." Jase Atwood accepted the handshake and then another one from Brad, before clapping his friend's shoulder. "Where's Jordy? If I've got to stare at your ugly mug, I need her beauty to counteract the effects."

"Here I am." Jordyn exited the bedroom, where she'd changed into black leggings, a T-shirt, and sneakers—definitely not an "I'm on vacation in the Caribbean" look. It was more of an "I'm an assassin on the hunt" look. "And you know better than to call me that. It's bad enough Carter does, but *him*, I have to put up with—you, I don't." Despite her words and annoyed tone, she walked up to Jase and gave him a friendly hug and a peck on his cheek. "Didn't think we'd be seeing you again so soon, but I'm not complaining. Welcome to the party."

"Thanks for the invite. All right, fill me in."

As they took seats around the suite's dining table, Brad studied the newcomer. In his midthirties, he stood about six one and carried around two-hundred pounds of solid muscle. Dressed in cargo shorts and a T-shirt, he blended right in with the island's tourist population. His light- brown hair was just long enough to skim the neckline of his T-shirt, and his mocha-colored eyes didn't seem to miss a trick. From what Carter had told him, the man was a mercenary of sorts and a contract agent of Trident Security, a Florida-based company comprised of bad-ass operatives, most of whom had come from the US military's special-ops community. They also had other employees who'd come from the varying alphabet soup agencies employed by the government, such as the FBI, ATF, DEA, NSA, etc. Trident was one of the best private-security companies in the US, and their multiple governmental contracts and successful mission rates were a testament to the fact. Brad and Avery had met one of the two brothers who owned the company at the party when Frisco had proposed to Haven. Ian Sawyer was a sarcastic son of a bitch, and Brad had liked him immediately. Sawyer was a bit of a legend in the Navy SEALs. Although most of his missions were classified, it was a good bet most of the rumors about his remarkable actions, leadership, and heroics on some hairy missions were probably true. Several of his SEAL Team Four teammates had followed him and his brother Devon into the private sector, having no doubts the new company would be a success. If Trident employed this guy, Jase, and Carter and Jordyn were also vouching for him, that was good enough for Brad.

As they finished filling Jase in with what little they knew, Carter's phone rang, and he answered it after a quick glance at the screen. "Reardon, tell me you got something." He paused then snapped his fingers and gestured that he needed a pen and piece of paper. Jordyn slid both toward him, then started typing on the laptop in front of her. "Repeat that name . . . Uh-huh." He jotted down the information he was receiving, and Jordyn glanced at it, before returning to her computer. "Address . . . Aliases? Relatives?"

"Got the photo Kenny sent me," Jordyn announced.

Brad, Cameron, and Jase got up and stood behind her, looking at the image on the screen. Jordyn glanced up at Brad. "Recognize him?"

Staring at the older Asian man, Brad shook his head. "Never seen him before in my life."

"Me neither," added Cameron. "Who is he?"

Carter disconnected his call. "Lin Chao. A man with a huge axe to grind and nothing more to lose other than his life."

"I'll be happy to take care of that last item for him if he's got Avery and Lori," Brad said with a growl. Strangely the man's name tickled his memory. He'd heard it before but couldn't grasp where.

Folding his arms over his chest, Carter read from the paper he'd written on. "Sixty-four years old. Former Chinese national. His empire, built on illegal trade, crumbled in the aftermath of his son's death."

Paling, Brad got a queasy feeling in his gut. "Oh, shit." Everyone looked at him, but his horrified gaze was pinned on Carter. "You mean his son's assassination."

The spy frowned and nodded. "Yes. Avery's last mission."

As Brad ran a hand down his face, trying not to throw up, Carter's phone trilled again. This time he put it on speaker and set it on the table, so everyone could hear. "Gene, you're on speaker."

Director McDaniel, the man in charge of Deimos, responded, "Good. Colonel Barton, you have my sympathy and full support. We'll do everything we can to help get Avery and your daughter back."

Taking a seat, since his knees where shaking, Brad nodded even though the other man couldn't see him. They'd never met but had spoken on the phone several times during and immediately after the joint mission between Deimos and his Delta teams when he and Avery had met. "Thank you, Director, but I'd like to know exactly how we're going to do that."

Before the man could answer, there was a knock at the door, and he apparently heard it. "That should be your backup now."

Carter strode over, checked the peep-hole, then swung the door open, allowing two men to enter. One was blond, the other dark-haired, but both looked like they could kill someone in a variety of ways, then disappear into a crowd without anyone knowing what they'd done. Average height, average build, and no outstanding features helped greatly when working as an undercover agent. Carter shook hands with both as, over the phone, McDaniel made the introductions. "Colonel, this is Kell Brennan and Troy Dartmouth. Men, Colonel Barton is from the Army's Delta. He's in charge of the mission. Do what he says to get the women back, then hightail it back to your assignments."

Both men shook hands with Brad and nodded when he thanked them for coming, before Carter introduced them to Cameron and Jase. After the necessary pleasantries were taken care of, McDaniel said, "As Reardon and Caldwell told you, this is Avery's last mission coming back to bite us all on the ass. After Lin Delan was dispatched, his father, Chao, was devastated to the point his competitors were able to take advantage. Before he realized it, his empire had fallen. Those he'd had in his back pocket had newer and bigger worries."

"Why wasn't Chao taken out too, if he was such a problem?" Jordyn asked.

"The head of China's Ministry of State Security at the time knew all about Chao and Delan's activities, unfortunately his wife and Chao's wife were cousins. It was a family honor thing that kept him from ordering the death of either man, yet he was all too happy to let another government do his dirty work. Instead of being charged for his crimes, Chao was exiled under the conditions he would never attempt to return to China or enter the US and never go after the agent who'd killed his son. That last part was a purely political demand for reasons I'm not going to go into; they're classified and not relevant to what's going on now. Chao had reluctantly agreed with the terms of his exile, knowing the alternative was another assassin's bullet. However, one of Delan's men had taken photos of the embassy people in the area immediately following the kill. After greasing the right palms, Chao learned which of them had executed the hit. It was one of the reasons I green-lighted Avery's field resignation." Brad knew the other but wasn't going to repeat it. "In addition to son number one, Chao had a second—Lin Zheng. He was eleven at the time. In the aftermath, he was sent to live and study under a Shaolin monk. After that, he went to university and studied business. He now owns a resort on Aruba, and, from what we've been able to tell, although his father's money was used for the startup, he's the complete opposite of the old man. Zheng is apparently an upstanding citizen with no skeletons in his closet other than his blood relatives. Whether he's now involved with his father getting revenge, I don't have that answer."

"So where do we find Chao?" Brad asked.

"He's got no properties in his name. Everything is under Zheng, so your best bet is to start with him at the Trade Winds Resort."

He stood. "Let's go."

Carter's hand on his arm stopped Brad's beeline to the door. "Let me and Jordy deal with Zheng. You going in there looking like you're going to kill the man might not be the best way to deal with him, or even gain access to him. While we're talking to him, the rest of you can check out the other properties.

Reardon said there's three more—a warehouse and two estates."

Grinding his molars, Brad forced himself to act responsibly and not with the anger and fear coursing through him. Nor the feeling of wanting to run into a place and rescue his woman and daughter without a well-thought-out plan. That could result in any one of them being killed. The spy was right. Brad would never let any of his men go off half-cocked, and he always tried to practice what he preached. That didn't mean he had to like it, though. Lin Chao was the man holding Avery and Lori, of that Brad was certain, and that was the man he wanted to choke to death with his bare hands. He'd refrain from taking his frustrations out on anyone else—for now.

"I'M SORRY, MR. BURKE, BUT MR. LIN HAS A VERY busy schedule today. Without an appointment, I'm afraid there's no way I can get you in to see him. If you'd like, though, he has some time available tomorrow afternoon."

Carter stood before the middle-aged receptionist. He'd introduced himself using his main Deimos alias—Carter Burke, CEO of a successful import/export business—having dressed for the part after stopping at a high-end hotel's clothing shop. A white, short-sleeved, button-down shirt topped a pair of khaki pants and loafers, sans socks. His long hair was pulled back into a neat ponytail, and he'd shaved before leaving their hotel. Just your every-day executive conducting business in the middle of his vacation. Behind him, Jordyn was looking every bit the wealthy woman with an eye for business, as she studied paintings and photographs of the resort that hung on the walls of the reception area. She'd changed again and now wore a white, knee-length skirt, a red, sleeveless, silk blouse, and black and white, polka dot sandals, all with expensive, designer brands on the labels. Her long, dark hair had been put up into a loose bun, and a white, broad-rimmed, straw hat and the sunglasses in her hand completed the look. The sales clerk who'd helped them earlier had made a nice commission on their purchases.

"Hmm. I'm afraid that won't do. My wife and I are leaving tomorrow morning for the Philippines. I have some business there that can't be rescheduled. I was hoping to speak to Mr. Lin about a small island I've acquired over there. I want to open a new resort but wasn't impressed with the one I'd come down here to see. After looking around the Trade Winds, I'm very interested in talking to Mr. Lin about the possibility of entering into a partnership or joint venture for the purpose of creating the new resort. But if he's not available . . ."

The receptionist's eyes widened slightly before she glanced at the closed door behind her and then back to Carter. She stood with his business card in hand. "Um, I'm not sure if Mr. Lin has time, but if you give me a moment, I can let him know the reason you'd like to meet with him and the circumstances surrounding why it has to be today."

His smile grew while his blue eyes sparkled. "I'd appreciate that very much, Ms . . ."

"Martens," she finished for him with a blush. "Valencia Martens."

"Valencia. That's a very pretty name."

The pink on her cheeks deepened. "Thank you. Um . . . p-please have a seat, and I'll be right . . . um . . . back."

As the woman knocked and entered her boss's office, Carter turned to Jordyn who was smirking at him. "You could charm the panties off a ninety-year-old woman in sixty seconds flat."

Setting his hands on her hips, he pulled her in

for a swift kiss on the lips. "The only woman I'm interested in charming out of her panties shares my bed every night." His mouth found her ear, so he could add in a whisper, "And I don't have to charm her at all since she sleeps naked, so I have access to that sweet pussy whenever I want." He nipped her ear and reveled in the shiver that went through her. "Just wait until I get you alone after this is all over, love; I'm going to rock your world."

"Promises, promises."

He opened his mouth to respond, but Lin Zheng's office door swung open, and the man, himself, strode out. "Mr. Burke? It's a pleasure to meet you." He extended his hand, which Carter shook. "I understand you have a business proposition for me."

"Yes, I do, and please, call me Carter. I thank you for seeing me on such short notice, but time is of the essence." He wrapped his arm around Jordyn's waist and pulled her to his side. "This is my wife, Jordyn. Your beautiful resort caught her eye, and she insisted we come to see you before we left the island."

Zheng took Jordyn's hand and kissed the back of it, before releasing her. "Then it is you I must thank. I'm honored the Trade Winds is to your liking.

Please, come into my office. Can I have Valencia get you some coffee, water, soda?"

Carter eyed his "wife" who shook her head. One of these days he'd convince her to tie the knot with him, but for now she was wearing an antique engagement and wedding ring set they'd purchased to use on a prior mission when they'd needed to be married for their cover. His gaze returned to Zheng. "No, thank you. We're good."

"Great." He gestured for them to walk into the office ahead of him. As he shut the door again, Carter strode over to the large window overlooking the resort and ocean, while Jordyn continued perusing the photos that also hung in the man's domain.

Zheng glanced between the two as if unsure which one he should butter up to first. Carter solved the problem for him when he shook his head and let out an appreciative whistle. "This is some view you have every day. If most of my business didn't take place in urban settings in the US and Europe, I'd have an office with a view just like this."

As he'd intended, he drew Zheng's attention away from the door, which Jordyn subtly locked while the resort owner strode to join his potential associate at the window. Carter circled the desk and took a seat in one of the guest chairs in front of it, casually resting the ankle of one leg on the opposite knee. Zheng followed his cue and sat in the leather, executive chair across the desk from him. As Carter began his fake business-proposition spiel, Jordyn slowly worked her way around the room until she was standing at the window, just over Zheng's shoulder. While the man was listening to Carter intently, Jordyn flicked her wrist and set the very sharp edge of her switchblade against his neck. Zheng froze, his face contorted in fear and confusion.

Carter remained seated and narrowed his eyes. "I'd keep your hands where she can see them, and your mouth shut, Mr. Lin. She's very adept at slicing a man open before he knows what happening. Obviously, we're not who you thought we were. Allow me to fill you in. Your father is holding a friend of ours hostage somewhere, probably with the intent to torture and kill her. We're very fond of the woman and will do whatever it takes to make sure she's returned to her loved ones unharmed." Zheng's face drained of blood, but Carter continued. "You clearly know who I'm talking about. Well, on top of taking this woman he wants revenge on, he's also taken an innocent young lady whose own father is ready to call on the hounds of Hell to rescue them both. We will not be leaving this island without them—alive —and I personally don't care who's left bleeding when we're gone. Nod carefully if you understand me so far."

Zheng's gaze slid to the side in an attempt to see the cold steel he could feel against his skin before he slowly dipped his head once.

"Very good. Now, I'm going to ask you a few questions, which you'll answer in a normal tone of voice. You will not do anything to alert your staff or security that there's a problem in here. If you try, I guarantee you'll suffer a painful death . . . after we get what we've come for. Understood?"

The man gulped then licked his dry lips. "Y-Yes. I understand."

"Where would your father have taken them?"

"Please, I—I didn't know—"

Carter's expression grew more ruthless. They didn't have time for the man's begging. "Where are they? One of your properties? The warehouse? Here at the resort? Where, Zheng? Don't try my patience."

When Jordyn pressed the blade harder against his neck, just shy of breaking the skin, the man stuttered. "H-His estate. H-He wouldn't have brought them here or to my home. The resort's storage warehouse has too many people there at this time of day.

The only place he could have the privacy he'd need is his estate."

"Who else would be there?"

"H-His bodyguards. He probably gave his house staff the day off."

"His mistress?" They knew from Reardon's intel reports, Zheng's mother had passed away about eighteen months ago, allowing Chao to continue the affair he'd been having for several years out in the open.

"No, she doesn't live with him. It's only my father, and his staff and guards there now. Please, I can help you."

"Why?"

His brow furrowed. "Why would I help you?"

Carter nodded. He had a pretty good idea what the man would say, but he wanted to hear his version.

"Because, I may be his son but I do not follow in his footsteps. I abhor everything he's been involved in, everything he is. I curse the day I was born to such a vile bastard. My brother was no better. My father may have given me the money to create the Trade Winds—I couldn't get that amount of funding without experience or backing—but I've paid him back. Every cent. The Trade Winds is no longer associated with blood money, and I will always regret that it was to begin with. I will help you get your friends back, but my father must never know I was involved. He won't care that I'm his son any more than I do, and he'll kill me. I would like to spare my wife and children from knowing my own father murdered me."

Having interrogated hundreds of people in his career, many under torture, Carter knew when someone was lying to him. Zheng was not. Carter nodded to Jordyn, who removed the blade from the man's neck, then stood. Zheng believed what he'd said, but Carter didn't want him to have a change of heart somewhere down the line. "If you double-cross me, you'll wish your father *had* killed you."

Zheng had sagged back into his chair after he'd no longer been in immediate danger of having his jugular sliced open, his hand going to his neck to check for blood. "Understood."

"Let's go."

CHAPTER 12

"YOU SURE WE CAN TRUST HIM?" BRAD EYED LIN Zheng, who was tapping away on his cell phone, in doubt, not completely convinced the man would help them rescue Lori and Avery. It wouldn't be much of a surprise to find out they were walking into a trap. While Carter and Jordyn had been doing their thing, Brad, Cameron, and Jase had checked out the warehouse, while the other two Deimos operatives had gone to Zheng's house, which wasn't far from the Trade Winds Resort. Brad and his team had just about confirmed the women were not at the warehouse when Jase had gotten a call from Carter telling them to respond to Chao's residence. Minutes later, Brad's own phone had chimed. Back in Texas, Col. Sheppard and Capt. Nielsen had been on speaker, checking in and seeing what they could do to help, which hadn't been much—not from that distance. Brad had assured them he had backup, of the black-ops variety, and hopefully that would be enough. He didn't think his teams could get down to Aruba in time. Chao had to know he was fighting the clock. He wouldn't be able to keep Avery more than a few hours without risking her being found on his property. As it was, the man had no idea who he was up against—but it wouldn't be long until he did.

"Ninety-nine percent," Carter responded while pulling a black T-shirt over his head to cover his bare chest. He'd left his khaki pants on but changed into a pair of soft-soled military boots. A few feet away, in a grove of trees near Lin Chao's estate, Jordyn had somehow managed to change back into her black leggings, sneakers, and T-shirt without flashing the men anything other than the back of her sports bra. Brad had never understood how some women could change outfits in the middle of a crowd without breaking any indecency laws.

"And what happens if that one percent blows up in our faces?"

Carter grinned. "Then I'll admit I was wrong." He clapped Brad on the shoulder. "Don't worry. We'll get the women out of there. Then Jordy and I will have a . . . chat with Chao. She has a new interrogation technique she's been wanting to practice."

Brad had no idea what intel they'd be trying to get out of the bastard, and he really didn't care. All that mattered was getting his wife and daughter back. His brain seized. Had he really just thought of Avery as his wife? As the seconds ticked by, he realized it felt right calling her that, and when he got her back, he was going to make sure she knew it. Brad had never thought he'd get married a second time, but, then again, he never thought he'd meet a woman who could handle what he did. She knew the life he led, what he'd done on past Delta missions, even if she didn't know the specifics. They both had terrorists' blood on their hands yet were still able to see the good that was out there. Avery was a woman he could grow old with, who would understand when he was having a bad day and couldn't talk about it. She was a woman who *got* him, and that was just what he needed.

"All right, let's go over this. I want no screw ups."

Carter rolled his eyes as if to say he never screwed up, but Brad couldn't give two shits. This was a team he'd never worked with before and, for the first time in years, he was terrified to go on a mission. Thinking about any alternative to recovering both women unharmed ripped his gut apart.

Stepping over to the hood of one of the SUVs they'd driven to the estate, Carter moved a small rock that'd been holding down a piece of paper with a map of the property crudely scribbled on it. "Zheng is positive Chao wouldn't have brought the women into the house; he wouldn't want to soil it with their blood—it's a religious thing, though I can't imagine Chao being holy. So, we're looking at this building here at the back of the property—a hurricane shelter built by the previous owners to accommodate a large family for several days. Zheng's only been in there once or twice a few years ago. From what he can remember there's six or seven rooms. Back then, there were some cots, shelving, and other crap, but he has no idea what's in there now. There's an entrance here and here," he said, pointing to the opposite ends of the long structure, "and only two of the rooms have windows—both hurricane strength so they won't shatter if they're shot at with the ammo we have; they'll only crack. Reinforced steel between the concrete is probably what's preventing us from getting the signal from Avery's tracker, in addition to the satellite glitch."

"How do we know which one to enter? Or are we

hitting them both at the same time?" Cameron asked.

Zheng held up his cell phone. "My father's bodyguards might protect him, but some of them are loyal to me. The job pays well, but they hate how he looks down on them as peons. I pay a few I know I can trust to report back to me. I texted one of them; he's currently standing guard outside this door here." He indicated the east end of the building on the map. "The younger woman is in this first room and unharmed, aside from some minor injuries from the accident. The other woman is down the hall and around the corner in one of these two rooms. I'm afraid my father has been . . ." He gulped then looked Brad dead in the face, his eyes filled with remorse. "He's been extracting his revenge. She's still alive but most certainly injured. The guard said my father and the head of his security, Shao Yan, are currently in the main house, but they'll be returning soon."

Brad's hands fisted. He wanted to hit someone—anyone—but there wasn't any time for that. He'd get his own revenge soon enough once he had Lori and Avery safe. He'd agreed to let Carter run the show, since Brad knew he was having a hard time thinking objectively—another first for a mission.

Pointing at Cameron and Kell, Carter said, "You two are in charge of getting Lori out. Zheng, you'll get them in there, and remember my promise—you double-cross us, and you'll beg for death." Carter must have drilled that into the other man's head since it didn't seem to faze him. Anyone else in the civilian world would probably have been shaking in their boots if the spy had glared at them while issuing the unveiled threat. "Is the guard at the other entrance one of yours or Chao's?"

Zheng shook his head. "You'll need to take care of him; he's a new guard and I don't know him well, other than to know I don't like him."

"Fine; he's expendable. Any guards inside?"

"No, there's just the two on the outside. I'll receive a text if someone goes in."

"Okay, Troy, Jase, that guard is yours. Take him out and make sure he doesn't come back to bite us in the ass. Brad, Jordyn, and I will take the door as soon as you're done. After you dispose of the guard, clear the rest of the rooms, then help Brad get Avery out and to the clinic." McDaniel had texted Carter the address of a clinic on the island with a doctor who would treat Avery and anyone else wounded in the rescue. He'd also keep his mouth shut in exchange for a large sum of money—they'd used him in the past and trusted his greed enough to use him again. "Cam and Kell, if Lori doesn't need a doctor, get her back to the resort and lock her down until you get the all clear. Jordyn and I will deal with Chao and his right-hand man. Zheng, after they get Lori out, you're done. Tell your guard to hightail it out of there only *after* your father and Shao come back and go inside—they'll know something's up if he's missing before that. Then, you head back to your resort like nothing's happened. Act surprised when the cops show up—and they will."

Brad noticed there was no longer remorse or regret in Zheng's eyes as he stared at Carter. There was something else—acceptance. "They'll be informing me of my father's death, yes?"

Crossing his arms, the spy nodded. "Yes. If you have a problem with that, tell me now. There are other ways I can make him suffer for what he's done, but he'll never be able to tell anyone what happened to him."

"That would mean I'd have to take care of him until his dying day; I highly doubt he would give me the same courtesy. I will be appropriately surprised when the police arrive." The man turned and stepped away, probably trying to come to terms with what he'd just agreed to.

"All right. Let's do a comms check." Carter hit the microphone on the headset he wore. Jase had brought a bunch of them in his bags of toys. If there was one thing Brad had learned about the Trident Security operatives, they came loaded for bear.

Once they were sure they were all connected, they disappeared into the heavy foliage surrounding the estate. As he followed Carter and Jordyn, Brad prayed like he'd never prayed before.

LORI SAT ON THE HARD FLOOR, SHIVERING DESPITE THE warm, muggy air in the darkened room. She had no idea how long it'd been since Avery had been taken. It seemed like days, but, in reality, it'd probably been only an hour or two. In addition to her throbbing shoulder, Lori's throat and right hand were killing her. After the door had slammed shut, and she'd found herself alone, she'd pounded on the steel and shouted at her captors. She'd demanded to be let go, begged for Avery to not be harmed, cursed the bastards who'd elicited the shrieks of pain from the older woman from somewhere in the building, and then prayed Avery was still alive after all had gone silent. Lori had only stopped yelling and beating on the door when it'd swung open and the tall, bald man pointed a gun at her chest. His short sentence had contained venom, glossed with the absolute truth. "Shut up or die."

She'd complied, partly from fear, partly from the wise advice her father had given her often while she'd been growing up. "If you're ever taken hostage, stay calm and bide your time until you can gain the advantage to escape. Look around you; find a way to alert someone. If you're in the trunk of a vehicle, feel around for the release or kick out the brake light cover and wave your hand out the hole. Find a weapon; anything can be one if you think about it. If you have to, disable or kill the bastard. Do it, then run. Don't look back. Don't worry about any conse-quences. Then call me and let me know where the body is so I can bury it."

Lori had always thought that last line was just her father joking, but now she wasn't so sure. She knew who he was in the military—Bradley "Tank" Barton was Delta. That meant something to anyone who'd ever heard of the elite team of soldiers. Deltas would do whatever it took to complete their mission. They were the Army's badass, black-ops team. The take-no-prisoners men who'd give their lives to save a teammate or an innocent. And now, as an adult, she had no doubt her father knew where some skeletons were buried, probably far more than anyone would ever know.

Daddy and Cam, please find us. I love you both so much. Please give me a chance to tell you that in person.

A faint click had her picking up her head as light filled the room again. She blinked several times until she could focus on the Asian man who'd furtively entered. Her eyes narrowed when he held up a finger to his mouth in the universal gesture of "stay quiet." He motioned for her to stand and walk toward him. His face was filled with kindness, sympathy, and worry—definitely not what she'd seen on the other men's faces earlier. Lori struggled to her feet and warily closed the distance between them, keeping her left arm against her chest to ease the pain in her shoulder. She was just about to ask him who he was, hoping he was here to rescue her and Avery, but he disappeared back out into the hallway. The door opened a little wider, and she realized the man hadn't been alone. Lori's eyes went wide as her heart pounded in her chest. Relief coursed through her, and she couldn't help the word that escaped her louder than she'd meant it to be. "Cameron!"

Her lover and a third man, whom she didn't

recognize, had stepped inside the doorway. Unlike the first man, these two were dressed from neck to toe in black with dark camo paint covering their faces, but it wasn't enough to prevent her from knowing instantly who Cam was. The large, black pistol in his hand was probably not the only weapon he had on him—not if her father had anything to do with the rescue, which she was sure he did. The second camouflaged man held an assault rifle and kept his attention on the door and hallway, while Cameron eyed her up and down, as if trying to convince himself she was really there and okay. He whispered, just loud enough for her to hear, "Sh, baby. Be very quiet. Are you hurt? Can you run? If not, I'll carry you."

Stepping into his side, she hugged him tightly with her good arm, feeling safe for the first time in hours. She lowered her voice. "I'm banged up, but I can run. But we have to save Avery. I don't know what they've been doing to her, but it isn't good. She was screaming—"

"Don't worry. Your dad and the others will save her. Right now, you're my only concern—we're gonna get you out of here. This is Kell; if he or I tell you to do something, you do it without hesitation. Got it?"

He didn't have to tell her twice. "Yeah. Got it."

Lifting her head, she met his gaze, and the emotion she saw in his eyes rocked her soul. He stepped back toward the door and held out his hand for her to take. "I love you, baby. No matter what happens, know that that's a fact. Now, hold onto my belt and don't let go unless I tell you to."

She did as she was told, then whispered, "I love you too, Cam. I always will, and that's a fact."

Kell spoke for the first time. "If you're all done with the declarations of endless love, can we get the hell out of here before the shit hits the fan?"

CHAPTER 13

AVERY'S WOOZY MIND SPUN ONE WAY AS HER BROKEN and bruised body rotated in the other direction. Her wrists were bound together and hanging on a hook in the ceiling, her feet about six or eight inches from the floor. Since all her weight hung on them, her arms and shoulders shrieked in agony. Her ribs and kidneys weren't faring much better. Yeah, her legs and back were hurting too, basically, everywhere the old bastard had struck her with a leather belt. Maybe she shouldn't have laughed at his first, weak punch, directed at her mouth. It'd hurt, but nowhere near what he'd probably intended. He must not have realized his age had caught up to him. Avery's days of being trained to withstand torture had come rushing back to her mind as she'd been dragged from the other room into this one. The problem was, like her assailant, she was much older now, and that training had been a long time ago.

She'd been careful not to piss Lin Chao off to the point he took his anger out on Lori. As long as Avery could keep him focused on her, the younger woman was safe—for now.

How long she'd hung there, practically naked, Avery didn't know. There were no windows in the room, only a single overhead light, a small table, two folding chairs, and an empty shelving unit—none of it within reach. Chao had beaten her for what seemed like hours, while his bald watchdog observed. He'd been the one to strip her down to her underwear, tie her wrists, and lift her onto the hook. Then he'd stood back while the old man had his fun. Avery tried hard not to scream when the pain became too much, but it'd been unavoidable. Thankfully, Chao had eventually tired and taken a break, the two men leaving her alone, which allowed her to take stock of her injuries. But they'd be back. She hadn't needed Chao's verbal oath to know her beating would continue after he got his second wind.

Part of Avery knew Brad would find them, but the other part worried he might not make it in time. Chao had no intention of letting her walk . . . or crawl out the door when he was done with her. Nope. He was determined to make her suffer for as long as possible before ending her life.

Was there a heaven? Would she be allowed in after all she'd done in her life? Avery didn't know, but prayed she'd somehow redeemed herself in God's eyes—if he existed. She was still up in the air about that, despite her Catholic upbringing. There'd been many times she couldn't reconcile the idea He existed after she'd seen all the evil that roamed the Earth.

Brad's face appeared in her mind. Avery had never thought she'd find "the one." She'd heard many women talk about finding theirs or read about happily ever afters in the romance novels she favored. But having gone over three-and-a-half decades into her adult life without finding hers, she'd figured they'd been the proverbial "two ships passing in the night." Then *he'd* walked right through her door—well, actually, Haven's door. Avery just happened to be in her charge's home at the time. Bradley Barton had marched in with confidence, authority, and a swaggering, rock-hard body that had made her swoon like a schoolgirl. Following a successful end to the mission they'd all been a part of, Brad had joined them for dinner, having accepted Avery's invitation. After he'd left, Frisco had teased Avery—apparently, she'd been drooling over Brad.

She'd been surprised when the object of her ogling had called the next day and asked her out on a date. Their second dinner together had gone a lot smoother for Avery than the first. Although she'd still had butterflies in her stomach, she'd been able to draw upon her training and act like an adult instead of a wide-eyed school girl with her first crush. After walking her to her door, Brad had gently kissed her on the lips, then promptly asked her out on another date. Two nights later, they'd ended up in bed together. Never had anything felt so right. So, why was this happening now? Had she gone decades without finding love, only to have it ripped from her grasp after a few short months? She hoped not.

The door to her prison swung open, and Chao strode in, looking refreshed, followed by his body-guard, who shut the door once more. The older man picked up the belt he'd left on a small table in the corner of the room. "Recovered from our first session yet, Ms. McNamara?"

Avery dug deep into her mind, body, and soul, and summoned a strength she hadn't needed in years. Her jaw ached as she snarked, "Absolutely. What's next on the agenda?"

An ugly snarl erupted from him as he stalked around her. "Bitch! You'll be begging for death soon. When you murdered my son, it was over in seconds. I promise you, your fate will not be the same."

He let the leather belt fly, and it struck her right hip. Pain bloomed instantly, and Avery choked on a cry. She tried hard not to give him the satisfaction of knowing how much it hurt, but, like before, she knew it would get to the point where she couldn't control it. Involuntary tears welled in her eyes, and she slammed them shut.

Chao hit her again. And again. He punctuated each blow with vile insults in both English and Mandarin. An especially-hard strike landed across her shoulder blade, which was already heavily bruised and lacerated, and, this time, Avery couldn't stop the howl that escaped her.

The door flew open with a loud bang, and three figures, dressed head to toe in black, skirted the jamb. The first one into the room fired a 9mm bullet into the forehead of the bodyguard before he ever had a chance to draw his own weapon. Despite his age, Chao moved quickly, using Avery as a shield. He suddenly had a gun in his hand and held it to the flesh covering her left kidney. If he shot her there, it was almost definite she'd bleed to death before she could get to a hospital.

"Let her go, Chao."

Avery would have sagged in relief if she could have at the sound of Brad's voice. Despite the black face paint, she recognized Carter, who'd killed the guard, and Jordyn as being the two people with him. All three had their weapons pointed at Chao. Unfortunately, Avery was blocking their shots.

"No!" Avery felt Chao's spittle hit her aching, bare back as he yelled in rage at the interference. "If I die today, I'm taking this murdering cunt with me! Either way, she'll never leave here alive!"

POUNDING IN HIS CHEST, BRAD'S HEART THREATENED to explode. He was so close . . . so close to saving the woman he loved, but it wasn't enough . . . not yet. He knew Lori was safe—Cameron and Kell were already on their way to the vehicles with her. Soon, she'd be back at the resort, safe in Cameron's arms. The man had proven himself in more ways than one over the past few hours, and Brad would gladly give his blessing if the couple decided to get married. The young Marine would have moved heaven and earth to save Lori, and that was enough for Brad. Knowing his daughter was safe allowed him to focus all his attention on saving his own woman.

Avery was hanging from the ceiling, her nearly bare body covered in welts and bruises. Her face was coated in sweat and tears. He caught a flash of relief in her eyes, underneath her pain. Fury shot through him. Lin Chao was a dead man—he just didn't know it yet. No, Brad would never murder the man, but when a moment of justification presented itself, and he was sure it would, then he'd take full advantage of it.

While Jordyn stayed just inside the doorway, Brad sidestepped further to his right. Carter did the same, but to his left. Jase and Troy were clearing the rest of the rooms to make sure there were no surprises the team had missed.

"You've got the wrong woman, Lin," Brad said, doubting he would believe the lie, but it was worth a shot.

The man's face was red with rage. He spat what was probably a curse in Mandarin before switching to English. "She murdered my son!"

"Let her go, and you'll walk out of here alive."

Another lie. "We'll leave your island and never return."

"No! She will never leave this island! I *will* avenge my son!"

Why Chao hadn't already shot Avery, Brad didn't know, but it was giving them a chance to save her. He needed all his attention aimed at the man holding a gun to her back. But what he really wanted was to look her in the eyes and let her know he'd do every-thing he could to get her out of this mess. There was no way he was going to lose her to this devil, hell bent on revenge.

Chao closed the distance between him and Avery, trying to keep her between him and the three weapons aimed in his direction. It suddenly occurred to Brad—despite his vow to die, taking Avery with him, the bastard wasn't ready to leave this earth. He wanted to celebrate and gloat after he killed her—something Brad would never let him do. "Do you really want your life to end right here? You were able to keep a lot of your money after you were exiled. I think a man as greedy as you would want to live long enough to enjoy every blood-red cent you made at the expense of others."

Brad shifted again to the right. There was no way he could fire his weapon. While he was certain he could hit Chao dead between the eyes, he couldn't risk the man pulling his own trigger. The bullet would rip Avery's kidney to shreds, and she'd bleed out very quickly.

"I don't care about my money! I don't care about anything except killing her! She took my son! I loved him more than anything in this world, and she murdered him!"

"Let her go, father."

Brad's gaze flittered to the doorway, then back to Chao, whose eyes had gone wide at the sight of the newcomer. Zheng took two steps into the room, his voice eerily calm. "I'm sorry Delan died. I'm even sorrier knowing you wished it was me and not him. I wasn't your firstborn. In fact, I should never have been born, but you thought the laws of China didn't pertain to you. You just paid someone off, so mother was allowed to have me. Why? You didn't want me. I often wondered why you didn't put me in an orphanage. All my life, I lived in Delan's shadow, even after his death. And now I'll have to try to explain to my children why their grandfather is dead. But I'm not sure they'll even care. You ignored them as much as you ignored me."

Brad had no idea why Zheng had come back after helping free Lori, but Chao was so focused on his son he seemed oblivious to the fact Brad and Carter had inched further around the room. They needed one second, one split second, when Chao's gun wasn't aimed at Avery. The rage on Chao's face increased tenfold. "You worthless piece of shit! You're right. I wish you were dead instead of Delan. He was my firstborn. My golden child. My legacy. You will never be even a tenth of the man he was. Never!"

Zheng shook his head sadly. "I thank Buddha for that. Now let her go."

"Never!" He pushed off Avery and stepped back, bringing his gun hand up and pulling the trigger as Brad fired his own weapon. Chao's head snapped back, blood and brain matter splattering the wall, and his body fell to the ground.

"Avery, no!" While the thunderous shots echoed throughout the room, Brad rushed forward, desperate to reach the woman he loved. She was swinging from the force of Chao pushing her, and she cried out in pain. Grabbing her around the waist, he lifted until her bound wrists cleared the hook. Her arms dropped as she sagged against him. He quickly but gently lowered her to the floor. "Fuck! Where are you hit?"

He tossed his weapon to the side, then ran his

hands over Avery, trying to find the gunshot wound to staunch the flow of blood. She couldn't die. *Damn it! Where the hell did the bullet enter?*

Avery hissed, then gasped in pain. "Not . . . hit." Her raspy words didn't register right away over the ringing in his ears. "Brad, I'm . . . not hit."

"Barton." Carter tapped Brad's shoulder and repeated his name several times until he finally looked up. The spy pointed toward the doorway where Jordyn was tending to an injured Zheng. The man had been shot in the arm, but, from the looks of it, would survive.

Brad returned his attention to Avery, his panic lessening when he found her staring up at him. He grasped the back of his shirt and yanked it over his head, before using it to cover her bare breasts.

Her hand found one of his. "I—I knew you'd come. J-Just glad you . . . made it in time." She swallowed hard. "Do me a favor?"

He brought his other hand up to softly stroked her head and face, needing to touch her but not wanting to cause her any more pain. Tears filled his eyes as he wished he could take away all the agony she must be in. "Anything, baby. Anything you want, it's yours."

"Take me home."

EPILOGUE

"You may now kiss your bride," the minister said with a grin.

Cheers and applause erupted from the occupants of the small church as Frisco, dressed in his formal uniform, wrapped his arms around Haven's torso, dipped her, and then kissed the ever-living heck out of her. The former undercover agent had been able to shed her wheelchair for the ceremony, and Carter had escorted her the short distance from the back of the chapel to the altar, before giving her away. Aside from saying "I do," it'd been the one thing Haven had wanted more than anything—to be able to walk instead of roll down the aisle. She'd worked her ass off to get to that point. While she was able to walk again, she tired easily and usually split her time between using the chair and crutches, but with Carter's and then Frisco's support, she'd been able to get through the ceremony without the devices.

It'd been a beautiful wedding, and Brad clapped along with everyone else, but his gaze wasn't on the happy couple. It was on one of the two bridesmaids —his wife.

Nine months had passed since their vacation-turned-nightmare in Aruba where Avery had cheated the devil out of his perceived due. As they'd been preparing to transport Avery and Zheng to the clinic for treatment, Ghost, Frisco, and two other Delta operatives, Fletch and Truck, had arrived on scene. Gene McDaniel had gotten top-secret clearance for the four men to break air-speed records from Fort Hood to Aruba to serve as additional backup. His reasoning had been it was better to have their boots en route and not be needed, than the opposite, and Brad was grateful for the man's initiative. Truck had brought a medic kit with him, and IVs were quickly placed into both victims before taking them for further treatment.

Meanwhile, Jordyn, Carter, and Jase had stayed behind and sterilized the scene. The guns that'd been fired had been swapped out for the two Chao and his guard had in their possession. The serial numbers of the two throw-away 9mms had been filed off long before they'd been used that day. The covert operatives must've done a good job because an online newspaper article Brad read two days later reported that Lin Chao and his bodyguard apparently had an argument of some sorts. Both men had fired their weapons, fatally striking each other in the head. Lin Zheng had told the reporter he was devastated by his father's death, but wasn't surprised, given how violent the older man's temper could be. Chao had been known for belittling his employees, and it had been only a matter of time before one of them snapped. There would be no funeral, Zheng had stated at the time, just a private memorial as his father had requested in the past.

After being rehydrated, having her injuries treated, and receiving some heavy-duty pain killers, Avery had been released from the clinic with no record of her having been there. Brad, Jordyn, Carter, and the Deltas had immediately taken her to the airport where an unmarked Army KC10 tanker was waiting to fly them back to the States. As far as the airport authorities in Aruba knew, it had been an American Airlines passenger plane that had come to pick up several company executives after their vacation had been cut short.

Jase, Kell, and Troy had left the island on the same planes they'd flown in on. Before they'd departed, Brad had thanked them tremendously and told each of them if they ever needed *anything* from him, all they had to do was call. He'd forever be in their debt.

Once they'd heard Avery was safe and would be okay, Cameron and Lori had gathered their things, along with Avery's and Brad's, and met them at the airport. No one had been upset about cutting their vacation short. In fact, everyone had been relieved and anxious to touch down on US soil again. The whole flight home, Lori had checked on Avery as she slept, almost as much as Brad had. Truck had also stayed close by, monitoring Avery's vital signs as instructed by the doctor.

During the five-hour flight, Brad and Lori had sat down for a long conversation. The first thing he'd immediately realized was he was back to being "Dad" or "Daddy" for the first time in twelve years, give or take a year. While they'd always loved each other, the distance of several states had made their relationship strained at times. But those days appeared to be over. By the time they'd reached Fort

Hood and put Cameron and Lori on a plane at the Killeen-Fort Hood Regional Airport, en route to North Carolina, the father and daughter had given each other their blessing. Brad had admitted he was in love with Avery and planned on marrying her the first chance he got. He'd also told Lori he'd be proud to have Cameron as a son-in-law, as long as he could still drop hints about burying the Marine's body if he ever did Lori wrong.

As Brad had expected, Cameron had completed his training a few months ago and was now a member of MARSOC. His Marine Corps special-ops team was stationed out of Camp Pendleton in California, and Lori had moved out there about six weeks ago to join him. She'd gotten a job at a nearby tattoo parlor and was already getting noticed for her talent. Cameron had called Brad the other night to ask for permission to propose to Lori sometime today and had received it with full approval. Brad was anticipating a call from his daughter in a few hours, announcing she was engaged.

It'd taken Avery almost a month to recover from her ordeal. Brad had helped treat the wounds that'd covered her torso and legs, his anger simmering just below the surface as he'd gently applied antibacterial cream to each one. The bruises had gone from black and purple to yellow and green before slowly fading away. As soon as the last one had disappeared, Brad had taken a knee and proposed, wanting to start new, happy memories for them. Avery had enthusiastically said yes. They'd eloped two weeks later after Brad had managed to swing another week's leave—he'd rarely taken them over the past ten years, so his superior had been all too happy to grant it as a wedding present. Although they'd taken some flack about eloping from their family, friends, co-workers, and teammates, Brad and Avery wouldn't have changed a thing.

Brad had never looked forward to going home every night. He'd lived and breathed the Army and Deltas for years. But knowing Avery was waiting for him each day had him wishing the clock would move faster so he could get back to where he wanted to be more than his next breath—in his wife's arms.

The guests laughed as Frisco swooped Haven up into his arms and carried her down the aisle. The flower girl, Fletch's young daughter, Annie, wearing a white and gold dress and Army boots, skipped behind them. She was followed by Carter and the maid-of-honor, Jordyn, then Avery, who was being escorted by Frisco's cousin, who'd served as best man. Brad went down a side aisle and met Avery at the back of the church. As he tucked her into his side, she smiled up at him. "Hey, Shrek."

"Hey, yourself. Did I tell you how beautiful you look today?" She was wearing a gold, knee-length dress that hugged her curves, and he couldn't wait to peel it off her at home later, after the reception.

Her grin widened as they stepped out of the church. Two Delta wives were handing out little, mesh bags filled with birdseed, which was to be thrown instead of rice when the newlyweds made their grand exit from the church. Avery took one for both of them before answering him "Only three or four times. You're slacking. Usually you're up to seven or eight by this time of the day."

Brad laughed. "I didn't know you kept count. Let me see what I can do about rectifying that." He bent his head and brushed his lips against hers. Everyone else faded away. When she regarded him with that look in her eyes that said she loved him, he felt ten feet tall and bulletproof. "You're very beautiful today, my wife. More than yesterday, and less than tomorrow."

"I love when you get all romantic," she teased as she ran her palms up his chest to his shoulders. "And I know I've mentioned this before, but, damn, you're incredibly handsome in your formal uniform. It does something to me."

His eyes danced. He bent down until his lips met her ear and then lowered his voice, so only she could hear him. "Something like get you wet?"

"Mm-hmm. And very, very horny."

He barely held back the groan that tried to emerge from his throat. "Have mercy, Mrs. Barton."

"Never."

I hope you enjoyed *Cheating the Devil: Special Forces: Operation Alpha*. Please take a moment to leave a review. They are greatly appreciated.

OTHER BOOKS BY SAMANTHA A. COLE

THE TRIDENT SECURITY SERIES

THE DEIMOS SERIES

The Ultimate Price: Book 3—Coming Soon

THE HAZARD FALLS SERIES

Don't Fight It: Book 1

THE BLACKHAWK SECURITY SERIES

Tuff Enough: Book 1—Coming December 2018

STAND ALONE NOVELS

The Road to Solace

SPECIAL PROJECTS

The Trident Security Coloring Book

Word Search For Warriors: Authors For a Cause

ACKNOWLEDGMENTS

To Susan Stoker—Once again, thanks so much for letting me borrow your characters and for being such an incredible inspiration!

To my editor, Eve—Thanks for being there to bridge the gap between the first and final drafts! Love you!

To Judi—What more can I say than "you rock!"

To my PAs, Maria and Connie and the rest of the staff at Lucky 13 Book Reviews and News—thank you for all your help!

To my beta readers—Allena, Ame, Angi, Cathy, Charla, Debbie, Elizabeth, Felisha, Jen, Joanne, Katie, Milynn, Olivia, Rhonda, Susan, and Tawnya—Love you all!

To the Sexy Six-Pack's Sirens group—as always,

your continued support means more to me than you'll ever know!

To my readers—I hope you enjoyed Brad and Avery's story. Thank you for continuing to ask for more!

To Jess, Jules, Brandie, and Kelle—Now that I've finally met all four of you in person, our friendships mean that much more to me. Love you!

ABOUT THE AUTHOR

A proud member of Romance Writers of America (RWA), Samantha A. Cole is a retired policewoman and former paramedic who is thrilled to add award-winning author to her list of exciting careers. She has lived her entire life in the suburbs of New York City and is looking forward to becoming a snow-bird between New York and Florida someday. Her two fur-babies, Jinx and Bella, keep her company and remind their mom to take a break from writing every once in a while to go for a walk, which is the best way to deal with a stubborn case of writer's block.

An avid reader since childhood, Samantha was often found with a book in hand and sometimes one in each. After being gifted with a stack of romance novels from her grandmother, her love affair with the genre began in her teens. Many years later, she discovered her love for writing stories was just as strong. Taking her life experiences and training, she strives to find the perfect mix of suspense and romance for her readers to enjoy.

Her standalone novel, The Friar, won the silver medal in the 2017 Readers' Favorite Awards in the Contemporary Romance genre out of more than 1000 entries.

While the original planned stories for the Trident Security series have been completed, they have brought many opportunities for Samantha to spread her wings and bring her readers more characters and stories to love. Look for her new Trident Security Omega Team series, Doms of The Covenant Novella series, Blackhawk Security series, and more from the Malone Brothers series, in addition to several standalone projects.

Sexy Six-Pack's Sirens Group on Facebook

Website

Subscribe to my newsletter

All Author

Facebook
—www.facebook.com/SamanthaColeAuthor/

Twitter—www.twitter.com/SamanthaCole222

Amazon—www.amazon.com/Samantha-A.-
Cole/e/B00X53K3X8

Book Bub—www.smarturl.it/SACbookbub

Youtube—www.smarturl.it/SamanthaColeYoutube

Instagram
—www.instagram.com/samanthacoleauthor/

Pinterest—www.pinterest.com/samanthacoleaut/

Goodreads—www.smarturl.it/SACGR

Mary B Moore: Force Protection

LeTeisha Newton: Protecting Butterfly

LeTeisha Newton: Protecting Goddess

LeTeisha Newton: Protecting Vixen

LeTeisha Newton: Protecting Heartbeat

MJ Nightingale: Protecting Beauty

MJ Nightingale: Betting on Benny

MJ Nightingale: Protecting Secrets

Sarah O'Rourke: Saving Liberty

Debra Parmley: Protecting Pippa

Lainey Reese: Protecting New York

Jenika Snow: Protecting Lily

Jen Talty: Burning Desire

Jen Talty: Burning Kiss

Jen Talty: Burning Skies

Jen Talty: Burning Lies

Jen Talty: Burning Heart

Megan Vernon: Protecting Us

Megan Vernon: Protecting Earth

Fire and Police: Operation Alpha World

KaLyn Cooper: Justice for Gwen

As you know, this book included at least one character from Susan Stoker's books. To check out more, see below.

Delta Force Heroes Series

Rescuing Rayne (FREE!)
Rescuing Aimee (novella)
Rescuing Emily
Rescuing Harley
Marrying Emily
Rescuing Kassie
Rescuing Bryn
Rescuing Casey
Rescuing Sadie
Rescuing Wendy
Rescuing Mary (Oct 2018)
Rescuing Macie (April 2019)

Badge of Honor: Texas Heroes Series

Justice for Mackenzie (FREE!)
Justice for Mickie
Justice for Corrie
Justice for Laine (novella)
Shelter for Elizabeth
Justice for Boone

Shelter for Adeline

Shelter for Sophie

Justice for Erin

Justice for Milena

Shelter for Blythe

Justice for Hope (Sept 2018)

Shelter for Quinn (Feb 2019)

Shelter for Koren (June 2019)

Shelter for Penelope (Oct 2019)

SEAL of Protection Series

Protecting Caroline (FREE!)

Protecting Alabama

Protecting Fiona

Marrying Caroline (novella)

Protecting Summer

Protecting Cheyenne

Protecting Jessyka

Protecting Julie (novella)

Protecting Melody

Protecting the Future

Protecting Kiera (novella)

Protecting Dakota

SEAL of Protection: Legacy Series

Securing Caite (Jan 2019)

Securing Sidney (May 2019)
Securing Piper (Sept 2019)
Securing Zoey (TBA)
Securing Avery (TBA)
Securing Kalee (TBA)

New York Times, *USA Today* and *Wall Street Journal* Bestselling Author Susan Stoker has a heart as big as the state of Texas where she lives, but this all American girl has also spent the last fourteen years living in Missouri, California, Colorado, and Indiana. She's married to a retired Army man who now gets to follow *her* around the country.

She debuted her first series in 2014 and quickly followed that up with the SEAL of Protection Series, which solidified her love of writing and creating stories readers can get lost in.

If you enjoyed this book, or any book, please consider leaving a review. It's appreciated by authors more than you'll know.

www.stokeraces.com
www.AcesPress.com
susan@stokeraces.com

Made in the USA
Coppell, TX
03 August 2021

59923693R00105